Two Times Removed

Two Times Removed

An Anthology of Indo-Caribbean Fiction

Edited and Curated by
Tiara Jade Chutkhan

Two Times Removed

Copyright © 2021 Tiara Jade Chutkhan

First paperback edition May 2021

Book design by Chelsi Bhagan
Stories contributed by Ashley Anthony, Saira Batasar, Kamala Chan Anna Maria
Chowthi, Tiara Jade Chutkhan, Alexandra Daignault, Tiffany Manbodh, Alyssa
Mongroo, Savita Prasad, Natasha Persaud, Karimah Rahman, Suhana Rampersad,
Krystal Ramroop, Jihan Ramroop, Mari "Dev" Ramsawakh, and Alya Somar

ISBN 978-1-7777274-0-6 (paperback)
ISBN 978-1-7777274-1-3 (ebook)

www.tiarajade.com

For the Indo-Caribbean community that never saw themselves represented in books, magazines, TV shows and movies.

For the Indo-Caribbean men and women who have struggled with their identity.

For the Indo-Caribbean writers who continue to share the stories and history of our community.

For everyone who has supported this book from its beginning stages until now. I can't tell you how much I appreciate you.

For each of the talented contributors of this book, this project could never have come to life without you. Thank you for sharing your stories with me. It has been an honour and privilege.

Contents

"We inherit from our ancestors gifts so often taken for granted. Each of us contains within this inheritance of soul. We are links between the ages, containing past and present expectations, sacred memories and future promise." — **Edward Sellner**

Introduction

Two times removed. We are two times removed. For Indo-Caribbeans, our story is one that began almost two hundred years ago when hundreds of thousands of Indian men and women made the bold and brave decision to begin a new life in a new world—the Caribbean. Our ancestors traversed the dark waters, what they called the 'Kala Pani,' and found themselves in the islands of Trinidad, Guyana, Jamaica, Suriname and many more. This was the beginning of a new era, one that encompassed this Kala Pani identity, this new Caribbean identity and the Indian identity we began with. These indentured Indians had big dreams, they wanted to achieve more, do more, create a world they previously hadn't had access to. They didn't know it at the time, but they were creating a history and culture that would later develop into what we call Indo-Caribbean culture. The food they made in the barracks after long days on the plantation, the songs they sang in gatherings and on the ships, their language and dress, all of which they did their best to pass down. It was their resilience and sacrifice that paved the way for the stories we get to tell today. It was because of them that this book got to exist.

Being Indo-Caribbean has often been a source of confusion and otheredness for me, as I know it has been for others as well. I grew up having people always tell me I looked Indian, as in from India, despite my objection and explanation that I was Trinidadian and Guyanese. Surveys that asked you to check your ethnic heritage only recognized Afro-Caribbeans as Caribbeans and South Asians as Indians. I checked the "other" box for years. My heritage wasn't recognized, it was 'other.' The day I finally saw an Indo-Caribbean option, my heart jumped at the fact that I finally had a space where I could fit in. But the continuous battle with identity doesn't end with a little box we can mark with a number two pencil. For me, this battle went on well into my college years, and only in the past two years have I truly been able to discover and access the resources that would help me find community and understand my past.

It's no surprise that I love to read. Books are a source of knowledge, they allow us to escape and join the lives of the characters we read about. We follow their lives and stories, clinging on to the perfect selection of words and sentences that bring us to places we've never been before or to people just like us. I can recall maybe two or three books in my childhood and teenage years that were set in the Caribbean and featured Caribbean characters. While there was certainly literature out there for us, in the average public school library, you weren't likely to find much. I remember in my grade nine English class, my teacher gave us a choice of three books to read and subsequently provide a report on in the weeks after. One book was called *Green Days by the River* written by Michael Anthony. The book followed a young boy named Shell and took place in Trinidad. One of the characters, Rosalie Ghidaree, was Indo-Caribbean.

I remember being excited, thrilled, you name it, to see a book that reflected my cultural heritage. After years of reading books about white characters, it seemed like I could finally add a bit more value to the discussion than usual. Unfortunately, few of my classmates chose the book and those who did were confused by some of the language. Again, I felt very othered and very strange that I came from this culture that was so unrecognized by the people around me.

It wasn't until 2019, I discovered a very well-known book called *Coolie Woman: The Odyssey of Indenture* by Gaiutra Bahadur. This was a pivotal moment for me, and I was fascinated and obsessed with this history I held in my hand. There were accounts of women on indenture ships, their lives on the plantations, the honest reality of what life was for the women before me. The photos transported me to a time period I could barely fathom. Looking at these faces, these men and women staring back at me, it was overwhelming. In all my years of school, I never saw anyone who looked like me or came from where my family came from reflected in history lessons. But here they were; they were real and they were in my blood.

Like many Indo-Caribbeans, my grandparents immigrated to Canada in the 70s and 80s, looking to start new lives with better opportunities for themselves and their children. My parents, both children at the time, spent very little time in their home countries. Coming to Canada cut them off from the stories and history they might have learned if they had spent more time with family or attending school back home. Being so young, they never thought to ask questions about ancestors and where they came from. They knew very little about indentureship and couldn't offer me many answers. The bits and pieces they could offer were precious, and I held on tight to each of the stories and clues I was given, preserving them in my memory.

With the information I had, I took matters into my own hands, learning and searching on my own and sharing with them what I found. After reading *Coolie Woman*, I spent endless hours Googling articles and research papers on Indo-Caribbean history and identity. I read about the different regions indentured labourers came from, the names of the ships, the experiences on board, life on the sugar plantations and everything else under the umbrella. Once, I tried searching for my last name, curious if I'd stumble across anything. Of course, it was far-fetched, but in any research process I think you can never rule out anything until it's been proven.

Later on, my mom and I asked family members, and I was able to collect more small clues to my own family story. On my mom's side, my family likely came from Uttar Pradesh and Punjab. On my dad's side, India, but no specific location. My grandparents' great-grandparents were born in the Caribbean, so it was likely that ancestors on both sides of my family immigrated during one of the earlier waves.

As you will see later on in the book, my short story is greatly inspired by my experience. My goal was to capture a snippet of the journey I went on through a character who was equally determined to learn more about her family and history. It was also this journey that inspired this book.

For those of us born abroad, in this case, North America, we carry a complex, hybrid identity. This identity consists of our Indian roots, our Caribbean heritage and our North American upbringing. These identities have greatly influenced our experiences considering most of us are either the first generation born abroad or immigrated with our families at a very young age. We grew up having access to technology, environment and opportunity that our parents and grandparents didn't. While our North American identity is such a large part of our lives, so is our Caribbean heritage. Many of us struggle to balance the two, holding on to visits back home, stories shared, music and food to keep us connected to a land and culture we haven't experienced to the fullest.

As you will see, each of the stories in this book reflect the experiences of young people in North America, but they also illustrate how Indo-Caribbeaness has played a role in those experiences. Things like bringing cultural dishes for lunch at school, people not recognizing our culture and grouping us in as South Asian, and navigating relationships with strict parents who want us to focus on school. After reading older anthologies, I found that the stories told often reflected the back home experience or that of someone newly immigrated. We are now part of this new genre that showcases the lived experiences of the first generation. While we will always need to preserve the stories of the past, I wanted to make room for the current stories and those of the future. They are equally part of our history.

I truly believe that storytelling is a talent and power that the Indo-Caribbean community has been blessed with. Our ancestors did not always have the privilege of reading and writing, but it never stopped them from passing on information. While much was lost along the way, there is plenty we can recover when we ask the right questions and open our ears to those who are accessible to us. It's our job, our generation, who will continue this legacy and keep the history alive.

As you read through each story, I encourage you to think of your own experiences, those of your friends, your cousins, your parents, your grandparents and look for the connections. I hope you will feel inspired to share your own stories and those of your family. There is so much comfort to be found in listening to one another and realizing that we aren't alone in our struggles.

I leave you all with a collection of photos, my inspiration, and this collection of stories, which I hope will be your inspiration.

A Conversation with Ajee

Suhana Rampersad

"Darling, you goin' and go to school or get married?" Ajee asks me earnestly.

My eyes go wide. I can't believe she's asking me this, I'm fourteen. Sitting beside her on the couch of her Chaguanas home, I lean forward to make sure she hears me.

"Ajee, I am going to *school*," I declare as clearly as I can, so her hearing aid will register. I almost roll my eyes; tanties are always trying to get girls married. I brace myself for a lecture on the duties of a daughter, the importance of full wombs and the fear of rotting eggs.

Ajee nods. "That is very good, you must always go to school," she pats my thigh and smiles.

What? I stare at her. She absently stares ahead, seeming to have already forgotten what she said. Her plump, drooping arms lean on her wide thighs while her aged hands lie in the lap of a blue house dress.

It's quiet for a few moments. Surprised by her response, I keep opening and closing my mouth, unsure how to reply.

Suddenly, she turns to me. "Yuh still dancin', Meera?"

I blink twice. "Yes, actually—"

"EH?" her face scrunches up.

"I SAY 'YES' I STILL DANCING."

"Oh ho, that is very, very good," her voice is high-pitched and raspy. "Yuh know, I used to take yuh fadda and dem to Ram Leela and Carnival, to weddings and ting. I used to sing in Ramayana and get on in di maticoor!" she laughs, coming alive at the memory.

"For true?" I smile back, imitating the accent. I want to know more about her earlier comment, but she's so joyful, I leave it for now.

"Yes gyal! I loved to dance and sing. Carnival used to be real nice back then, with music and pan and pretty, pretty costumes. Now it have all kind of naked gyal with they little piece of clothes, now it not so nice," she swats her hand, dismissing the festival like a mosquito.

I chuckle at her old-fashioned resolve and reach for my phone on the coffee table.

"I might have a video..." my words trail off as I flip through my photo library, passing the many pictures from this trip. Ajee leans in and watches intently as my fingers glide across the screen with speed.

"Aha." I click on a performance video and hold the phone out to her. She looks at it, then to me, her brows furrowed, neck drawn back. I nod, "take it."

She hesitates, but takes the phone. "I doh business with dese fancy gadgets, yuh know." She holds the phone in one hand and tilts her chin up, holding her head far back and the phone far forward.

The screen reflects in her glasses. Little translucent versions of me twirl and step, moving in the glass mirrors before her eyes. The sound of shimmering ghungroos play along to an old Hindi song.

Ajee's smile grows wider and wider as she watches. A warm feeling, proud but shy, spreads in my chest.

Other than the video, it's quiet, so I decide to make conversation. I don't know much about her, but I love to read, so maybe she does too.

"Ajee?"

"Hmm, chile?" Her eyes remain on the screen.

"What's your favourite book?" I fold my hands.

"Book? Me, I never learn to read," she states flatly.

"...What?" I whisper.

She lightly kisses her teeth. "Back then they never really used to send girl chil'ren to school. So I never learn..." she shrugs, her cheeks drooping slightly, her lips in a straight line.

I looked away, trying to hide the pity I knew screamed from my eyes. This is all new to me. I don't know what to say.

She continues watching the video, and soon her little smile returns. The performance was a lengthy classical one I knew she'd like. She says she loves to dance, but I wonder if she's ever had the chance to train. Probably not, so I decided against asking. Though, I don't really know what else to talk to her about.

As she watches the screen, I observe the room. The coffee table is a smooth brown, with small chips here and there. On top is a bowl with the green remnants of bhaji and roti, the result of visiting on one of Ajee's fasting days. The couches are floral patterned, pink with hints of grey and green. The cabinet in the corner holds a clunky TV, topped with old souvenirs from her few visits to Canada. On yellow painted walls, dozens of photo frames hang, some slightly tilted, as if she had to put them up herself. There's my uncle Jai's wedding photo. My parents standing in the snow. My cousin Shiva and our late grandfather sitting by a bedi for prayers. Me and my cousin Asha when we were little, hugging, our faces squished together. Our family is anchored here on Ajee's wall.

The photos make a myriad, and at its center is a sepia seeped image so small I can't make it out. I stand from the couch as Ajee continues watching my dance, and step closer.

The photo is old, matte, and slightly crinkled. Still, I recognize Ajee in a plain saree, standing next to Aja in a kurta. It looks like their wedding photo.

She looks very young, very familiar too. I narrow my eyes and look closer. Actually, with that baby face, she looks a lot like me.

Over my shoulder, I ask, "Ajee, how old were you when you got married?"

"EH?" She turns away from the phone.

I join her again on the couch, this time sitting on the arm of the chair, repeating my question.

What she tells me stuns me.

Ajee was married at fourteen. *Fourteen.* She had her first baby two years later, in a wooden home with a man nine years her senior. In a flash of time, there were seven boys and one stone pot to feed them. She spent her school years as a wife and mother, as expected of her.

How did I not know this before? I barely knew this woman. Memories of avoiding phone calls appear like a weight on my brain.

Ajee pays no mind to my silence. She looks down at the phone again. The performance has already ended.

"You does dance real good chile." She adjusts her glasses and hands back the phone.

I slowly take it from her.

She coughs, then pushes against the couch to stand slowly, painfully. "I goin' in de kitchen for some watah. Yuh want some sweet drink?" her voice squeaks on the last word.

I'm numb. "No, I good, thanks."

She wobbles through the living room and into the kitchen.

I sit there. She must've thought marriage vs. school was a dilemma I was facing, since it's what she faced. *I* had just graduated grade eight, and my grad present was a trip to Trinidad. Soon I'll be in high school, then university. Marriage was not something I had to worry about for a long, *long* time.

Yet at my age, Ajee had already been a bride. She'd been working the land, knuckles deep in soil, planting cocoa and selling produce to feed her boys. *I'd* been gallivanting from house to house, visiting family, going to the beach, to MovieTowne and to the market.

From fourteen on, all she had was her faith, the pitch in her voice and the honour of a family. All she must've wanted was to go to school.

I feel pangs of guilt.

The sound of pans clanging in the kitchen grabs my attention. I watch Ajee's stiff movements as she puts two pots to boil on the stove.

She looks up and sees me watching her, then gives me a gummy, sweet and almost comical smile. "Yuh want tea, Meera?"

I manage a half-smile. "No, thanks." I rise from the armrest, "Um...yuh need help with anyting?" I ask, twiddling my fingers.

She squints her eyes and tilts her ear in my direction. "I does cyan hear too good gyal...wha' yuh say?"

I enunciate, "Do- you- need- help- with- any-thing?"

"Oh! Yes, come and wash up dese wares for me," she points to the sink.

I head into the kitchen, joining her by the sink. Picking up one of the plates, I start scrubbing. Ajee toddles about, opening and closing cupboards while packing things away.

It's quiet as we both do our work. The dishes scrape and clink as I pick up, lather, and set them down in mechanical motions. Above the sink, the kitchen window is open. The early evening breeze flows in, brushing and waving the white doily curtains. The kitchen tiles under my feet are cool.

As I'm washing, my mind wanders. When Uncle Jai dropped me off this morning, I dreaded having to spend a few nights by Ajee's house. I have never known how to connect with her. I have never enjoyed talking on the phone with her, since she could hardly ever understand what I was saying. Visiting her always felt like a duty. Having to miss out on KFC was another factor, since Ajee fasts almost every other day. I could've been with my cousins right now, having fun.

Only now, I feel like I've missed out on getting to know her. My own grandmother who was a child bride. I thought things like that only happened in places like India, not Trinidad. There must be so much history, pain, and tragedy. I wish I knew more, and had more time to learn. She's getting older, who knows when she'll go? When she does, everything that she knows, all the little details about our family history I never thought to ask her about, will go with her.

I turn the pipe and listen as the water rushes onto the stack of plates, trickling from edge to edge, like a layered fountain. I rinse, then lie the plates face down on the red towel next to the sink. While drying my hands, a low humming starts up. It's a song, a familiar tune, but I can't place it. Behind me, Ajee has ducked below the counter, packing away pots. When her head bobs up to reach the basin, sound emits from her closed lips.

I slowly turn around and lean against the sink, following the softly rising sound as it turns into singing. Her song is steady, clear, inviting. I can't remember if I've ever heard her sing before.

Ajee approaches the stove and sings as she stirs the pots; one of boiling milk, the other, tea. A folded fist rests on her hip while her lips move in tune to a Hindi song. The music reverberates in her throat, smooth even at the highest note. Her voice is like Lata Mangeshkar, she pulls to and fro every note in perfect pitch and tone. The sound travels from her mouth, wafting amongst the steaming pots.

I watch, imprinting this moment into my mind. Taking snapshots of her stance, records of her voice, memorizing the joy in her feet as they tap, the twirl in her wrist as she turns the pot.

It dawns on me that she is the last of us to know Hindi. I cast my eyes down. My gaze falls upon her tapping feet. They are small, stout, neat in shape, with a high arch, and very familiar.

I look at my own. Huh, we have the same feet.

I watch her hands, mannish and veiny. I notice the shape, the strong thumb bones like a chiseled jaw. They're the same as my dad's, same as mine.

What a strange resemblance to share. A thought kindles.

Her feet that wished to dance are the same ones that got to spin on stage with me. Those hands that turn silver pots have written tests and poetry, read aloud to the whole class.

I've got to do it. *For* her. Far away in foreign land, I lived out her hopes and dreams.

Sighing in relief, I feel a peaceful sleepiness. It's like I'm small again, and she's singing to me.

"Darling?" She breaks the tune.

"Hmm?" I hum, eyes half-closed.

"You could go lie down in the room if yuh want," she chortles.

My eyes fly open. I push myself off the ledge and stand straight. She's started pouring tea and milk from the pots into two mugs. I shake my head and smile. She made me one anyway.

I approach the counter and take the two mugs in hand. She looks at me.

"That's ok Ajee," I say, motioning to the living room. "Come, let's keep talking."

Chatterbox
Kamala Chan

I still wonder how she did it. My mother, eyes dark like night, skin gold like honey, packed up her only two belongings and brought us to a land so foreign the people were colder than the snow. Berbice was minuscule and '*Merica* was the largest dream she had. She walked an hour each way to work because the rice and curry in our bellies meant more than the corns on her feet. My mother, eyes dark like night, skin gold like honey, flew 2646 miles away from all that she knew so I could be all that I am. Even when all that I am seldom makes sense.

We lived in the Bronx, New York, a large Caribbean community. My Ma and Nana (grandparents), mousies (maternal aunts), mamus (maternal uncles), and cousins all lived in our neighborhood. Respectively, we were raised with Guyanese culture thick like the *dhal* Mommy cooked on Sunday mornings. We didn't talk about our emotions in our household. Mommy didn't talk to me about fear, anxiety, depression or self-doubt. She didn't talk to me about struggle. She especially didn't talk to me about pain. I was expected to get straight A's in school and was generally punished when I didn't meet her expectations. *Two lix* were all it took for me to do my schoolwork. I loved reading and writing, but the pressure of having to be perfect pushed me away from trying in school.

"Ayo get am too good in dis country," she would often exclaim. The gold bangles on her wrist jangling as she places her hand on her worried forehead.

One of my first memories of realizing how much we didn't talk about important things is when I got my first period. I didn't get any warning about what changes my body was going to experience. In fact, at eleven years old, I thought I was bleeding to death when I saw a random splotch of bright red blood on my ruffled white cotton panties. She handed me over to my older cousin, who gladly talked my ear off about what was happening. Later that evening, I overheard her on the phone with my aunt.

"Gyal, me can't believe, meh baby yuh turn young lady suh soon."

I still wonder why I didn't deserve a conversation about our shared divinity.

That experience led me to reflect on other moments when we didn't communicate. Like the time Daddy left us to move to Queens; I was just seven and my brother thirteen. We didn't talk about how she felt. We didn't talk about how divorce is looked down upon in our community. We didn't talk about how we were going to mend a broken family. We didn't talk about how hard my brother took the burdens of that loss. We didn't talk about how he struggled to focus in school or build and maintain relationships.

We didn't talk about how confused I was to no longer be his baby girl, his "little" as he once called me. We didn't talk about how the harsh realization that those hands, callused from cutting Guyanese cane and building American houses, was no longer there to safely guide me across the busy New York streets. Those hands, calloused from cutting Guyanese cane and building American houses, were miles from being the tender touch of a Father, wiping the tears that came with bruised knees and broken hearts.

Weekend visits became monthly visits and monthly visits became holiday visits. As my relationship with my father faded, I delved into my mother's mindset. I learned to understand that she chose to not dwell on hardships.

"Every fowl feed pon he own craw," she'd tell me.

Meaning, everyone has to learn what is good for themselves eventually. She didn't have time to talk about her problems when there were mouths to feed and lives to live. This woman is the actual life of the party. An aura that outshines the Phagwah parade in Smokey Park. *My Tassa queen is hotta than a plate ah Cook Up* and has a heart as pure as Guyana gold. But we didn't talk. Talking prevents, talking helps and talking heals.

I did my best to fit in with my very American peers at school while following the strict upbringings of my Caribbean mother. I was eager to befriend the same kids who made me feel ashamed of the coconut oil on my head and the hair on my arms. So, I learned to adjust. I stopped oiling my hair on Sunday evenings and wore long sleeve shirts all year round. If there's one thing I learned from my mother, it was to adapt.

I'd chatter all day with my friends in school and go home to my fictional ones in books. Mommy got calls from school about my chatterbox mouth. I'd have to hear the routine, "Gyal, you guh run meh pressha up. Teacha say yuh talk whole day."

My reasoning behind this was socializing with friends outside of school was absolutely not allowed. In fact, if I saw my male classmates in public, I'd look the other way.

I vividly remember asking to have a friend over once.

"Ma, my friend Nicole invited me over, can I go?"

"Gyal, nah tek yuh eyes and pass me," she sucked her teeth.

"Okay, well can she come hang out here?"

"Hang out where? Not in dis house! None Merican pickney nah come in me house wid shoes. Dese chiren nah get no manners and house training."

"Mommy, please!"

"You like yuh wan me geh yuh something feh cry fa."

She kissed her teeth again and went back to washing her Gilbaka fish with lime. That was that. End of conversation.

I came to understand that back home in Guyana, your friends were your family and your neighbors. She didn't realize that I was brought to a country where friendships outside of school were significant for a child's development and social skills. As I got older, she became more lenient with friends. Of course, we never talked about it, it just sort of happened. Talking prevents, talking helps and talking heals.

I experienced my first anxiety attack in my early twenties, already married. I had no idea what was happening and why it was happening to me. Soca Brainwash was a huge Fete held in the heart of Brooklyn. It was in the middle of July and we were in the middle of the crowd. It. Was. Lit! A melting Pepperpot of my beautiful Caribbean people. In every direction, there were flags waving and waistlines pelting. Then suddenly, it happened without warning. The energy was delectable, but mine was distasteful. The music was loud, but my thoughts were louder. My husband and friends were at arm's reach, but seemed so distant from where my mind wandered. How did I feel myself caving into darkness on the brightest day of summer?

I soon learned that some of the main causes of social anxiety are overprotective and restrictive parenting along with traumatic childhood experiences. Experiences like your parents getting a divorce and never really taking the time to explain why. Although I make friends easily, I often find myself unable to trust the intentions of the people around me. I overshare now and overanalyze later.

I'm still searching for balance. I'm still developing the social skills that I was unintentionally deprived of in my adolescent years. I'm still learning that it's okay to not always be okay. It's normal to feel anxious in an unfamiliar crowd. It's normal to be cautious of who you trust. I learned that most of us grow up not knowing enough, talking about enough, or coping with enough. We have to be the change we want to see in future generations.

I found myself searching for understanding. So naturally, I turned to books. I read books on psychology and books on mindfulness. I read books on self-accountability and books on social adaptability. I'm constantly searching for ways to teach myself about myself. I write just as much as I read. I strongly believe that daily reflection is the key to growth. I know my mother did the best she could in raising me, but it's my turn to re-parent my inner child.

Ironically, one of the main strategies that helps me is talking. My chatterbox mouth is always up for a conversation on self-love, self-advocacy, and self-discovery. I have countless bar conversations with strangers on the subject. Living with anxiety seems to be the furthest thing from strange these days. It's our body's natural reaction to stress after all. I embrace the values that I learned growing up in an Indo-Caribbean household with thick accents and strict rules. I also embrace the values that I'm learning living in an American city with tender conversations and forgiving hearts.

My relationship with my niece, Vada, is built on a strong foundation of understanding and communication. Since she was comprehensive, we've been having open conversations. I am proudly the canvas she paints the colors of curiosity on. We're best friends. So much so that she refuses to call me Aunty. When she was just five years old, she gave me a short but blunt explanation of why I should be addressed on a first-name basis.

"Mommy didn't give me a big sister, so I'm taking you."

No argument there.

She holds a certain wit and charisma that mirrors my childhood self. Her long, thick, black hair drapes down her petite back, as mine once did. She has a fruitful mind and a colorful wardrobe. She represents both the future and the past. We read books that highlight what it means to be brown in this country and how special it is that we are so beautifully blended. We talk about how women are treated differently from men. We share moments of joy through understanding. We experience each other through pure conversation.

This is why talking holds so much significance in my life. As women from a culture where we are often censored, uplifting each other gives us a voice. Lack of conversation is common in our culture. Our mother's struggles are different from ours and we must understand before we assume. We must teach the next generation what our parents didn't have the luxury of doing; as they did for us what their parents couldn't have done for them. That is our purpose as immigrant children. Our stories hold so much power. For me personally, generational trauma does not determine who I am and the life I continue to build. Especially when my mother, eyes dark like night, skin gold like honey, spoke such volumes with her silence.

Cups of Tea

Mari Dev Ramsawakh

Nadya watched the steam rise from her cup. She was too tired to do anything else; not watch TV, not read, not finish her work, not unpack. There were boxes stacked around her, some half-opened with their contents spilling out onto the floor. But all she could do was watch the way the steam curled upwards from her drink. She had made the tea as a comfort, but she knew there wasn't any relief to be found in her empty apartment.

She blew softly, momentarily dispersing the steam into invisibility before taking a tentative sip. It tasted exactly as it should have, but Nadya was right. There was no comfort in her warm cup. She put the cup back down on the coffee table and slowly slid lower until she was curled up on her couch cushions. She stared at the solitary cup with empty eyes.

She wasn't sure how long she had been lying like that, when the sudden ring of her phone startled her. She groped around without taking her eyes off the cup of tea, likely lukewarm now, until her fingers curled around the buzzing device. Her mother's contact glowed across the screen. The idea to reject the call briefly tempted her. She was prepared to sit in this heavy aching boredom for as long as she could. But the instinctual fear of a missed call from her mother was enough to swipe that green icon as she uprighted herself.

"Hello?"

"Hi babe! I'm just checking in on you. I know you must be feeling lonely now that you're on your own for the first time." Nadya's eyes rolled at the unneeded reminder.

"I'm fine, mom. How are you doing?" She reached for the now definitely lukewarm tea, settling in for what she knew would be an unnecessarily detailed account of her mother's daily life to which she would make the appropriate sounds of acknowledgement.

"...So now I have to make something to go with the rice. Have you eaten dinner yet?"

"Not yet mom," Nadya answered robotically. "I will soon though."

"I get so worried about you there on your own. Are you sure that the building is safe? What if something were to happen?"

"Yes mom, the building is really safe," she answered in the same robotic tone. "You know, I should probably get started on dinner anyway."

"Oh right, right." Her mother's voice sounded soft suddenly. "Okay, I'll let you go. I just wanted to tell you how proud I am of you."

Nadya paused. She hadn't expected that last sentence to be so jarring. "What?"

"I've been thinking about everything you've been through and everything you've done. I'm just so proud of you," her voice cracked. "I watched you as a little girl, trying so hard to make everyone happy, and I really thought that *he* was going to make you happy. I thought he would be different from all the men we've known. I had no idea..."

"Mom, hey, stop. You don't have to say this."

"No I do! I look up to you, you know."

"Mom."

"I really do. You know, I was with your father for years. I didn't know any better. He wasn't as bad as— Well, he wasn't awful you know. I thought that was how marriage was supposed to be. I just thought he was around and that had to be better. I wish I could have taught you better, I just didn't know. You still managed to get out on your own, so much sooner than I did."

"It was different for you mom. I didn't have kids, it was a different time."

"Yeah." The line was quiet. "I just wish I could have been more like you."

"But I learned it *from you*."

"What?" Her mother's voice sounded incredulous. "All you could have learned from me is my anger and craziness."

Nadya laughed. "Exactly. You taught me how to stand up for myself. You taught me to make my voice be heard no matter what. And okay, sure, you didn't always handle it well, but your anger was valid. I couldn't have gotten out if it wasn't for the strength, resilience and independence you taught me."

"Really?" Nadya wasn't used to hearing her mother's voice sound so small.

"Really." She took a sip of her tea. Even cold, it suddenly tasted much better.

***

"Yuh wan some tea?" Her grandmother's Trini accent rang from the kitchen.

"Yes please!" Nadya called as she used her fork to mix the pools of dhal and bhaji into her rice. She reached across the table to pick up a little glass jar and sprinkled some pepper sauce across her food before mixing it in.

"Alright," her grandmother sighed as she set a cup in front of Nadya and eased into the chair across from her. "Why yuh don't come visit more often?"

"I've been busy, Grandma," she answered between bites.

"You been working?" Nadya nodded. "Yes, that's good. You should always be focused on your work. You should always be able to take care of yuhself."

"Yeah, I'm trying." Nadya hadn't mentioned why she moved or why she suddenly started to show up alone on her visits. Her grandmother never asked either. Most of the time she was grateful for that, but in this moment, she could feel the unsaid words hanging between them. Was this supposed to be a supportive comment? Was it an *I told you so* in disguise?

It was just the sound of their forks scraping against their plates as they ate for a minute. Then Nadya cleared her throat. "You've..." She stopped and started again. "Can you tell me about granddad? Mom doesn't remember him very much and I never really got to know him."

"Oh. Oh boy." Silence. Nadya frantically started to wrack her mind for a change in topic. "Your grandfadder. Yes you wouldn't know him. I didn't really know him myself."

Nadya spoke carefully. "How did you meet?"

"Uh, well, I used to visit my sister in San Fernando during breaks from school and while she was working she wouldn't let me cook. There was this popular restaurant, I would get my food then go sit down in the gallery and read a book. Your grandfadder would come up to me every day. When I would get up to leave, he would follow me and keep trying to talk to me. That's how we started talking. I liked talking to him and I felt sorry for him, but I didn't know that it wasn't love. It wasn't love."

Nadya tried to remember the last time she ever heard her grandmother talk about love in a relationship before. She wasn't sure why the idea surprised her so much. She knew that her grandmother was in a relationship, but it was always sort of unspoken around her. He was just another uncle around at her grandmother's who helped build things.

"What happened?" she asked quietly.

"I had your aunt and your mudder so fast. Eighteen months and I had two babies."

"And you were just a kid."

"Yes, I was only sixteen then. Your grandfadder, he liked to get dressed up and go to parties. I would have to stay home and just wait for him. I didn't like it. And he used to *drink*. We all used to drink sometimes, but when he drink he would cuss and throw food out the window and slap me." She sighed. "Oh baby. I been through so much."

Nadya reached over and took her hand. She had never seen her grandmother look soft or defeated before. In all of her life, she had always seen her grandmother as stern, strict and strong. It had never occurred to her that her grandmother could have started off any other way.

"And you been through so much too." Her grandmother squeezed her hand back before picking up her fork again.

Nadya picked up her cup and took a sip. The warm tea was oddly soothing to her spice-tinged lips.

***

The sun was warm and there was a soft breeze. Nadya squeezed past the glass door onto her mother's back patio. She set down a cup of tea in front of her grandmother and curled into a wicker chair with her own cup. Her mother followed closely behind with her drink and a plate of fruit which she set on the table between them.

"So Nads," her grandmother started, "How's work? Yuh always so busy, but it's good that yuh working a lot. It must be going well."

Nadya nodded. "Yeah, I'm starting a new project this week. I'm going to be busy again, but I can relax this weekend."

"What's the project?" Her mother piped up. "Is it something you've done before or are you learning something new?"

"A little bit of both." Nadya had always been a bit more reserved when she was with her family. She preferred to let them carry the conversation. But as she began to describe her difficulties with a new computer program, her voice quickened and she began to wave her hands emphatically.

"Yuh so much like yuh mudder," her grandmother said suddenly.

"What do you mean mummy?" her mother laughed. "I don't know how to do any of these computer things. I have to call her brother to help me all the time."

"But yuh always learning tings. Yuh both always trying to be something better."

"So are you mummy."

"Oh no, I don't learn nothing. These brains too ol now."

"Didn't you tell me that you were learning how to cook new foods lately?" Nadya reminded her. "You told me on the phone that you learned how to make that alfredo like how you buy it."

"Yeah mummy, you've always been learning for as long as I can remember," her mother added.

"I never think of it that way." Her grandmother smiled.

Nadya reached back to the table and picked up her tea again. She chuckled softly as her mother and grandmother started to bicker over a memory they both remembered differently.

Dear Divya

Saira Batasar-Johnie

Waking up on Saturday morning, Anjali heard the familiar sound of her parents listening to Ingrid and her father (who we all knew as "Uncle") updating the Indian & Indo-Caribbean community about upcoming events and news.

The smell of curry loomed through Anjali's bedroom. The soon to be fourteen-year-old was up late talking to her cyberspace friends on Habbo Hotel and MSN. Her immigrant parents had no idea it was a website where their young, innocent daughter could meet strangers and talk to them about anything under the sun.

"Anjali, wake up! Half da day done finish pikney," Anjali's mom yelled from the kitchen.

Anjali's mother, Seeta, was an older woman who had immigrated to Canada in her 20s during the Burnham period in Guyana. Seeta became an illegal refugee, living in hiding and working cash jobs. She couldn't return to Guyana because it wasn't safe. A neighbour had reported her and she had had to move quickly. Her friends knew of a single Indian man looking for a wife and she was able to marry the stranger to receive her papers and stay in Canada.

Seeta was the third eldest of her eight siblings and her childhood was very different compared to that of her daughters. She had a hard exterior and was often strict with her daughters, resulting in two rebellious teenagers. Seeta did not want her daughters in the kitchen, she wanted them in their books. But the girls had other plans. Her husband was not around often as he would work 12-16 hour days running the family business. The girls didn't see their father much, so she was often left to raise them on her own.

Anjali cleaned her recent nose piercing as soon as she woke up. She was proud to have gotten it done since her older sister Amara had gotten hers right before she started high school. It was like a rite of passage for her. Her mother left a basket of laundry to hang out. Anjali plugged into the latest Aaliyah CD on her discman. "Rock the Boat" blared through her ears as she ignored what her mother was saying and walked out of the house with the basket.

As she collected the laundry, Anjali practiced her dance moves and wondered if she would kiss a boy this year. She wondered if someone would notice her since she had lost weight and developed new found curves. If the girls that bullied her for smelling like curry, being hairy and having big hair would now admire her defined eyebrows and want to be her friend. Would she fit into high school the way her older sister did? She wondered if she'd meet other girls who looked like her. Anjali laid in her backyard hammock deep in thought. "One in a Million" started playing as she noticed Amara sneaking out behind her parents' back to meet with a boy. She wondered if she would soon do the same thing too.

***

It was the first week of high school and all Anjali could think about was her outfits. She wore big silver hoops with a tight black t-shirt, blue skinny jeans and new Baby Phat black and white sneakers. She reminded herself what Amara had said to her.

"Don't talk to me if you see me. Just keep walking."

Of course that had hurt Anjali, but she was used to her sister being mean one day and her best friend the next. Anjali's mom dropped her off at school. Her sister had a first period spare so she would arrive later that morning. Her mother spoke up as she got out of the car.

"Anjali, don't talk to no boys. Focus on your schoolwork, yuh hearin me?"

Anjali rolled her eyes and responded. "Yes maa."

Her mother waited and watched until Anjali entered the school before she left. When she opened the doors to her high school, all she could see was BOYS.

She saw her best friend Kristen and smiled instantly. Kristen had pale skin with freckles and had been Anjali's friend since the first day of middle school. They were both never in the "cool crowds" and Anjali didn't have any Caribbean or Indian friends. Aside from the one other Trini boy who purposely ignored Anjali because she smelled like curry and wore her hair in a long braid in middle school, there was no one else. Anjali was set on creating a new image for herself in high school. She was done being a "curry girl" and wanted to embrace her newfound curves, nose piercing and curly hair. That meant no more long plait braids. She was DONE being bullied.

Kristen and Anjali compared their schedules and had no classes together. It was devastating. Who was Anjali going to sit with? Talk to? She felt worried and nervous. They entered the cafeteria for grade 9 orientation and everyone from middle school looked at her as if she was a new person. Anjali noticed people from the other schools she had played in basketball tournaments. She and Kristen walked to a row of empty seats. A group of girls watched her up and down, but she brushed it off.

She wondered what Divya would have thought about first day jitters. It was something they used to talk about all the time.

Anjali longed for a boyfriend. Kristen had been with her boyfriend since seventh grade and she was constantly third wheeling with them ever since. No one wanted to date the Brown girl who was chubby with braces, had thick frizzy hair and ate strange food for lunch. Anjali had struggled with her appearance. She knew she didn't look like her peers; their blonde or brown hair, different coloured eyes, and skinny bodies. She wanted to look like them, but her mother forbade her to dye her hair or get coloured contacts.

The principal gave a final announcement before dismissing the students to their classes.

Kristen told her where they would meet for lunch, gave her a hug, and went on her way. Anjali checked her schedule and started walking to room 108 for Geography class. She had to walk through "The Circle" where all the cool kids were. She saw Amara who was beginning twelfth grade; her glowing dark brown skin and freshly straightened hair. Anjali's mom wouldn't let her use a straightener. She was scared it would damage her curls, which instead left Anjali to manage her frizzy hair on her own. Her mother didn't know what to do besides putting coconut oil in it.

Amara was being hugged by a tall, beautiful guy with smooth dark skin. *Wow, he's hot*, Anjali thought. They were surrounded by a group of people, laughing, and coupled up. To Anjali, they all looked like they were already in college.

Amara's eyes locked with Anjali's and she quickly pulled her in the circle.

"Damian wanted me to introduce you to everyone. So everyone, this is my little sister Anjali. Don't let shit happen to her, okay? Bye."

Anjali waved awkwardly and kept walking. Damian came up behind her.

"Hey, I know your sister is weird about you being here, but if you need anything, please don't hesitate to ask. High school can be really shitty."

"Okay, cool." She smiled.

Thoughts ran through her head all at once. *Oh my god, my sister is dating that guy. Oh my god, my sister is popular. Oh my god, does this mean I'm popular? Oh my god, Mom and Dad can never find out or we would both be dead! How is my straight A sister so cool?*

Anjali was floored at what she had just experienced. As she walked into her classroom, a boy named Kevin who teased her almost every day in middle school called out to her.

"Oh hey, look it's curry girl!"

Everyone giggled. Anjali told herself she wasn't going to put up with this bullshit anymore, so she responded to the taunt.

"Go fuck yourself Kevin since no other niner will."

"Go to the office!" the teacher screamed.

Anjali stormed out of the classroom and to the office. After waiting for a few minutes, the Vice Principal called her in and announced she would be suspended for two days. Her mother was already on her way to pick her up.

Anjali waited outside. She saw Amara and Damian and told them what happened.

"I'll deal with the kid," Damian said.

At that moment, Anjali saw him. He had brown skin, light brown eyes, plump lips and spiked hair. He had a line up around his chin connecting to his mustache. He wore baggy pants and a baggy white t-shirt. He rocked a Jansport backpack, fresh, white Air Force Ones, and a Guyana flag hung from his back pocket. He had his earbuds around his neck with a soca mix blaring from it. He. Was. So. Hot.

He shook hands with Damian. Damian looked at Anjali.

"Anjali, this is Naraine."

Before she could respond, Amara disappeared. Their mom had pulled up to the front of the school. Anjali never got in trouble at school, let alone be suspended. She was in for an ear full from her mother.

Seeta blazed her all the way home.

"Wah de mudda ass. How yuh so schupid? Amara never been suspended. Wait, you just wait. You are grounded. I takin' that blasted discman. Yuh tink you can ignore me, hmm? You can listen to some bajans and maybe God can heal you."

Seeta went on and Anjali tuned her out. All she could think about was Naraine. Did he even notice her? She wondered why Amara was being so nice to her. It was only the first day and so much had happened.

When they got home, Anjali went to her room and gave up her precious discman. She laid in bed, her heart thumping quickly. The thoughts in her mind made her feel hot and flush in her face. She reached for her journal and began writing.

Dear Divya ,

Today would have been our first day of school together and you would have loved it. There were boys everywhere; short and tall, fat and skinny, in all different shades—unlike middle school. There were even Brown boys! I was like, thank goodness, finally guys that don't go to temple that I can chat to. Oh yeah, I also got suspended and my mom is losing her shit. I wonder if Dad will even care or notice I exist. He has been extremely distant since you.

Remember Kevin? I swore at him and told him to go fuck himself. He called me a curry girl as usual. I have no time for bullying in ninth grade, I'm not having it. You wouldn't believe this either, Amara was nice to me at school. Remember she'd always say "don't talk to me in front of my friends" or would use us to get out of the house to go hang out with them. She's a completely changed person. I wonder if she and I will become friends. I miss when we were younger, when Amara started high school she became weird and "too cool" for us. AND she has a boyfriend! I think she's a badass considering we aren't allowed to date. She's dating the most popular guy in the school. She's so cool. I won't say that to her though, unless she's nice to me.

And then there was Naraine, who I looked like a total loser in front of today. He was this 5'11 body of gorgeousness. His eyes, and skin, no pimples. I hope I don't get any this year. Damian (Amara's man) was introducing me to him and my mom totally embarrassed me and started honking the horn. I wonder if he'll notice me again, or if he'll talk to me next time I see him. I wonder what cologne he was wearing so I can go secretly to the drugstore and buy it. Girl, it smelled so good. Like dreamy good. Like Nelly, take off all your clothes good!

LOL I'm being so silly. I hear my mom calling me to clean since there's no homework.

Dear Divya

I miss you.

Love,

Anju

Dig a Little Deeper

Tiara Jade Chutkhan

I-n-d-o C-a-r-i-b-b-e-a-n h-i-s-t-o-r-y

Click.

Various Google links popped up on the screen of Kavita's MacBook.
The first, a Wikipedia page that she couldn't resist clicking on—despite years
of school telling her the website was unreliable. She scrolled through the
paragraphs of information, fishing for key points that would answer the
plethora of questions swirling in her mind. Her eyes were burning from hours
staring at the screen. Nestled in the comfort of her white fleece blanket, she sat
with her laptop propped up on her lap and a warm Milo on the nightstand
beside her. She grabbed the tall glass and swirled the spoon around the
chocolate flavoured milk to redistribute the lumps of powder. The classic
Caribbean drink had been a staple in her home for as long as she could
remember. Her dad had gone through a phase with buying Ovaltine, but in
her opinion, nothing tasted the same as Milo. She always liked to sneak a
scoop of the tasty powder before mixing it with milk. She loved the chocolatey
grains melting in her mouth.

With some of her energy replenished by her drink, Kavita was determined to continue searching for articles and papers. She had been at it for a few hours already and was deep into her vortex of research. She wanted to learn anything she could about her people. The people she looked like, ate like, spoke like, but had been a mystery to her for most of her life.

An article written by an Indo-Caribbean student at an American university caught her attention. Kavita clicked the link and began to read. The student spoke of her experience growing up in a world that barely understood her—she also barely understood herself. Kavita nodded as she read. It was reassuring to know that others felt the way she did, but they were strangers thousands of miles away, and that did little to comfort her any further.

The sudden interest in her cultural heritage seemed out of the blue to her family, but for Kavita, it had been looming over her since her childhood. Now at twenty-three, Kavita found herself unable to move forward without knowing and understanding where she came from. She was curious about her ancestors, about their journey. She recalled many times in school where other kids would talk about their lineage, knowing of their ancestors that descended from European countries. She was envious of them; they knew several generations of their family tree, what those people did and what they looked like. She knew nothing, could trace nothing. Her lack of knowledge had been a constant bother, always knocking around and reminding her she didn't know herself as well as she liked to believe.

She scrolled through the images tab, marvelling at the first waves of Indians that graced the Caribbean islands almost two hundred years ago. Some of the women were adorned in jewelry, mostly gold. They wore bangles, stacked along their slim arms, and large nose rings with additional jewels dangling about. Kavita looked at her own jewelry box, filled with gold pieces.

The women she saw wore their thick, dark hair neatly parted in the middle, a traditional look it seemed, with long braids down their backs. Kavita twisted her fingers through her own long tresses that hung to her backside. In the night, she always braided her hair down her back to keep it from getting in her face while she slept. The similarities almost felt like a coincidence. Some of the women wore saris and head scarves, while others left their hair uncovered and wore simple dresses, likely for the long work days on the plantations. It felt foreign yet familiar at the same time.

Kavita's Indo-Caribbean heritage came from two places. Her mom was from Trinidad and her dad from Guyana. While most people would say to her, "*Aren't they basically the same?*" her mom always strongly pointed out that they were different. Kavita agreed for the most part. The two countries certainly had their similarities, but there were things indeed that made them different. Sometimes it was the name of a food, a custom, or a little detail about the way of daily life. Regardless, having to dig into the history of two countries only added to her list of searches.

The sound of a light knock on her door broke her focus from the screen.

"Come in," she called softly.

Kavita's dad, Rohan, walked into the room. She hadn't realized he was still awake.

"What are you still doing up pumpkin?" he asked.

Kavita looked at the time on her computer. It was after 1 a.m. and she hadn't noticed. "I've been researching. Dad, what can you tell me about our family?"

Rohan ran his hand over his bald head. "Well, you know my family is from Berbice. I grew up in the country and my grandfather owned all the land on our street. He gave land to each of his sons and they all built houses for their families. I think he rented a few houses to family friends as well. I was surrounded by family until I left to come to Canada with your grandmother."

Kavita was familiar with this part of her dad's life. Her grandmother had come to Canada to start a fresh life, leaving young Rohan in the care of her parents. When he was five, he left the Guyana countryside and moved to the bustling city of Toronto.

Rohan continued his story, "When I came to Canada, it was the biggest shock of my life. I came in February and as soon as I got off the plane, my grandmother tried to put a jacket and hat on me and I didn't want to wear any of it. We lived downtown, so suddenly I was seeing cars, stores and more people than I was used to. It took me a couple years to really get adjusted to Toronto as my home."

Kavita nodded. Her dad had often mentioned that coming to Canada was a difficult time for him. He went from being surrounded by family, eating fresh foods grown out back, running around barefoot with his cousins to navigating traffic, new foods and having few family members around. His grandmother had stayed in Toronto for almost a year to help him adjust before returning back to Guyana.

"What else do you want to know? I wasn't around long so I'm not sure I have the answers you need," Rohan said, taking a seat on Kavita's desk chair.

"I want to know about our ancestors. You know, the ones who came from India to the Caribbean. Do you know anything about them? Or if your grandparents' parents worked on plantations? I've been reading about indentureship all night," Kavita told him.

Rohan opened his mouth to speak when another soft knock on Kavita's door diverted their attention. Her mom, Stella, walked in.

"You two don't sleep? What are you talking about so late?" she said with a hand on her hip.

Kavita and Rohan told Stella about their conversation, extending the questions asked to her.

Stella took a seat on the edge of Kavita's bed. "Well, you know I was born in San Fernando. I'm the opposite of your dad, I'm from the city and was used to the hustle and bustle. My grandparents owned a supermarket that was across the street from my school, so I would run over and get lunch and snacks all the time."

Kavita pictured her mom as a child, dressed in a school uniform, her hair in two braids and her small hands digging into a bag of candy. Stella had often told her about all the sweet treats she loved eating as a child, missing the taste of them now that she was older. She hadn't been back to Trinidad in over twenty years; Kavita often wondered why.

"I was ten when we moved to Toronto. It was New Year's day when we landed and everything was covered in thick snow. I wasn't happy about it all, in fact, I hated it. I begged your grandma to let me stay back home, one of her sisters even offered to keep me. But no, she said wherever she went, her children would have to be with her. I had no choice but to adjust," Stella said.

Being born in Toronto, Kavita was used to the cold, the snow. She didn't like it, but she was used to it. She couldn't imagine spending the early years of her life knowing the hot sun, fresh fruits, crystal clear waters and tropical palms only to leave it behind. Toronto's four seasons, maple and pine trees and imported foods that never tasted the same as back home (so her parents told her), couldn't have measured up to what they had known prior.

"What do you know about our ancestors? I was asking dad just before you came in. I don't know anything about our family that would've come from India to the Caribbean," Kavita asked.

Rohan cleared his throat. "I don't know much about my family's side. My grandparents and their parents were born in Guyana. I do remember my grandmother had a tattoo on her arm, it was a mix of numbers. I had never thought to ask her about it, but she might have been branded when she was young."

Kavita noticed Stella nodding her head, looking away as her husband spoke. Something struck a chord.

"My great-grandparents also had some sort of number tattoo. I was too young to think anything of it as well. No one talked about indenture or our Indian roots. As far as we were concerned, we were Trinidadian, and that was that. I do remember my uncle once telling me we had a family member come from Punjab. My dad's grandmother was mixed White and Indigenous, specifically Arawak and Carib. That's all I know," Stella said.

Kavita's mind surged with the new clues her parents had provided. She hadn't read anything about branding or tattoos. She wondered how her family might have gotten those; she wished there were pictures and more stories.

"Is there anyone in the family we can ask?"

"I will call your grandparents and ask what they know," Stella assured her.

"I'll do the same," Rohan said.

Kavita thanked her parents for sharing their stories, gathering them both in a big hug. Two hours had passed since Rohan first came in to check on her and their eyes were all heavy with sleep. Kavita said goodnight to her parents, and they left, urging her to get some sleep and pick up on her research during the day.

As silence returned to the room, Kavita quickly opened her notes app, jotting down key words from her parents' stories.

"Branding tattoos...where did indentured servants come from...indigenous people of the Caribbean," she read to herself.

After finishing her list, Kavita shut her laptop. A long yawn escaping from her mouth. All of the energy her Milo replenished was now gone. She placed the laptop on her desk and slid back into the warmth of her bed. Her mind was still on everything that she had read and heard that night. It felt complicated, this whole history. Now that she knew more, she realized plenty of pieces of the puzzle were missing. But that's what they did, didn't they? Erase our history as well as that of many others. She went over it in her head. After slavery in the Caribbean was abolished in 1838, the British plantations owners sought out a new source of labour to replace the free Blacks. They turned to India, bringing hundreds of thousands of Indians as indentured labourers. They signed contracts that said they would commit to working in whichever designated island for five years on average. After that, they were promised tickets to return home to India. This never happened, with exception to a lucky handful.

What would make people want to leave their homeland to go somewhere strange and unknown? Many times in history this had been done, but for the first time, Kavita truly contemplated it. Her grandparents had left their homelands when her parents were children and moved across seas to

Canada. She knew why, for a better life, opportunities, the usual things she had heard many times. In the context of two centuries ago, she felt as if there was so much more that played a part. Things she may not necessarily be able to comprehend. Her parents had grown up in Canada and now her, a first generation born here, could never imagine having to make such a big decision.

Kavita wondered what it would've been like growing up in Trinidad or Guyana. She had heard stories from both her parents, but vivid as they were, she couldn't truly picture herself in the environment. North America was all she had ever known. She often hung out downtown with her boyfriend, on packed streets with shops and food everywhere. She had spent her teenage years in the mall like any other young person and despite hating the packed public transit with its smells and inability to ever be on time, she was used to the atmosphere. She was used to maple trees, pines staying green all year long. Even though her family had taken multiple tropical vacations, being on a resort wasn't anywhere close to what local life was like.

Another yawn cleared her head of its activity. It was almost four in the morning and even though she had no work or school the next day, she knew it was time to throw in the towel. She could resume the searching and questioning after her desired eight hours of sleep. Kavita pulled her blanket up and tucked her head between the fluffy covers and her pillows. She turned on her side and closed her eyes. Her dreams were filled with visions of lush greenery, indigo waters and bodies that came in all shades of brown.

Three days later
Kavita sat in the living room surrounded by photo albums. She had been fortunate to finish class early and was eager to move on to the next phase of

her research. Her mom told her there were some old photos buried amongst the heap of memories. Kavita had planned to save her search for the weekend, but couldn't resist the chance to find more of her family history.

As she leafed through the albums, she recognized many of the moments; her fourth birthday, her dad's thirtieth, a trip to Niagara falls, a day at Marineland. Over the years she had been through these albums plenty of times, but never with the intentions she had now.

She picked up the fifth; a thick, glossy album with a floral print. Flipping open to the front page, Kavita saw a young Stella in an array of 90s style outfits.

"Gwan wit yuh bad self Momma," Kavita said with a smile.

Midway through the album, she found exactly what she was looking for. Kavita carefully removed the photos from the thin plastic pockets, not wanting to bend or crease them. Photos of her mom, a baby, and her grandparents, young, stared back up at her. Her grandmother, no more than twenty-five she guessed, her hair a reddish brown, longer than Kavita's. Her grandfather, thin and dressed like an Indian movie star. She ran her hand over the photos, slightly tinted with age. *This was almost fifty years ago*, she thought to herself. It was a different time, different place, an era she would never know outside of these still moments.

She grabbed her phone, positioning each photo under the light and snapping a picture. She couldn't risk walking around with the originals, but knew she'd need them on hand to reference when she went looking for more stories.

Kavita heard the jingling of keys and looked up to see her dad was also home earlier.

"Kavi? You're home early," Rohan said.

"Hi dad. My class finished early, so I came home to dig through the albums. I found a bunch of pictures of Grandma and Grandpa."

Rohan shrugged off his jacket and hung up his keys. Kavita could tell he had something on his mind.

"I talked to your grandma today, and asked about the family," he began.

Kavita's heart raced. She prayed he was able to get some information, anything. Rohan took a seat next to her, moving the albums she had piled and placed them on the coffee table.

"Your grandmother's great-grandfather came to Guyana from India, though she's not sure exactly where. His name was Ragubar Singh; she thinks it was around the 1860s when he docked. Ragubar worked on a plantation for a few years before taking work on a ship. When he was finally able to settle, he took his savings and bought enough land to create a small village in Berbice. It began with his family and a few friends. Eventually, more Indians settled in the village, creating a real community."

Kavita's eyes widened at the short story her dad had just shared. She reached for her notebook, quickly jotting down the details she didn't want to forget. In her imagination, she pictured a man, hands calloused from hard work, skin burnt from long hours under the sun. Dressed in loose rags, a cutlass in one hand, determined to make something of this new life in a new world.

"You know, now that you've got your mom and I on this wild goose chase, I can't believe I never thought to ask your grandparents these things," Rohan laughed.

"Yeah, Dad, these things are important. Growing up, all the kids in my class knew their entire family trees and I knew nothing. I don't want these stories to get lost," Kavita said.

"You're doing a good thing, I'm proud of you," Rohan said, pulling her into a hug.

They both looked up, hearing the familiar jingle of keys in the door. Stella walked in, her face flushed.

"Hey hun, what—"

She interrupted before Rohan could finish, "I just got off the phone with Grandpa. You're going to want to hear this."

Kavita sat up, her notebook and pen firmly gripped in her hands. Whatever gems Stella had uncovered, she wanted to hear, to record. All these people that had come before her, that she couldn't have been here without, she was determined to honour them. To make sure another generation wouldn't have to be unsure.

"Pull up a seat, Mom, we've got all night."

Her Love Story

Alyssa Mongroo

She ran past her roommates, not even acknowledging them. Down six flights of stairs like a madman and out the door. They stared, confused by the hurry. The thick smog slapped her face when she opened the front door of her apartment building. Her eyes began to water, dark lines smudging her eyes like kohl. She shrugged it off because no brown girl was ever complete without her eyeliner. From the water's moisture, her orange toned foundation turned to cream. She caught herself before she took another step past the door and pulled out her phone.

The text on her screen read: *Be there soon.*

She glanced at the other bright numbers on her phone. The time. She realized there was no way she'd make it. What was she doing? She should be studying, focusing on her independence, not going to meet a complete stranger. She could hear the thoughts enter her head. They weren't unfamiliar. They were words her mother had spoken. Words her grandmothers both said. She knew she was lucky to even be in college, to even set foot on campus and get a higher education. But today was Saturday and she just wanted to have some fun.

"Why does it have to be a boy? Why can't you just hang out with your roommates?" her mom asked when she told her.

"Mom, we have nothing in common," she stated plainly. She didn't want to get into it with her mom. She was the only girl among her roommates in the engineering program at her school. Her roommates were studying teaching and had so much more to talk about. They would go on coffee runs together before preparing for their observations, laugh about the kids in their observation class, and talk about everything together. Well, everything that didn't concern her.

It was her first year in college. She was away from being coddled by her family and for the first time she had to learn how to be an adult. We all think adulting is easy when we're younger. We see our moms do it with such ease, cooking gourmet meals like curry chicken and endless round rotis, taking care of the children, cleaning so much that there isn't an ounce of dust left in the house. All such hard work, but they made it look so easy. They look so happy while they're doing it and at the time, it seems fun. We're all in such a rush to grow up; wishing we could go out and party like our older cousins, wishing we could wear that tight dress that we see women wearing at house parties. Yet when we finally become adults, we don't want it.

For the first time, she had to learn responsibilities; grocery shopping on a budget, remembering to make the bed in her itty-bitty dorm room, managing her time so that she could take care of her home. She couldn't cook curry like her mom, but she could make ramen noodles. Okay, more like heating them up. But with a bit of Matouk's pepper sauce stirred in for a nice, spicy kick, they began to taste like home.

That spicy closeness to home wasn't enough. She was lonely too. All her roommates were having fun with each other, and since there weren't many girls in her classes , most of her friends were boys. They were great, but they didn't understand her sometimes. She missed her family a lot. Whenever they were all together, her big Indian family, they had so much fun. There was endless food for your pleasure; banana flavored cola sweet enough to wash the hot spices away, and an array of desserts to fill your belly. She and her cousin would be talking about where they liked to go shopping, how school was, and boys. They'd take drives with her siblings and her other cousins to absolutely nowhere, just to get out of the house and away from the adults. The adults would be drinking, laughing, sometimes yelling about politics and back to laughing. It was a merry time when they all got together.

She missed that. She was so lonely away from her home. One night, a wine bottle later, she downloaded a dating app. She could hear her mom's disapproval from miles away. You can judge all you want, but we've all been there, we've all done it. She plugged in her information, her most gorgeous photos, and started swiping. Left, right, her tiny finger glided across her phone. Then she stopped. His picture stood still on the screen. He was so handsome. He stood tall and dark, his hair shaped nicely, his smile bright and white. She knew by his complexion he was Indian. She swiped, revealing a photo of him with his parents. They were dressed in simple traditional attire, and they all looked happy. There weren't any more pictures, so she proceeded to his bio. AUS Villimar College, Economics student. Plain and simple. He was an international student attending Villimar. Villimar was her school's biggest competitor and they also had the biggest study abroad program in the country. She knew he was real, he was in both pictures, so nothing seemed out of the ordinary. Her finger swiped right.

He probably won't swipe right back, he probably doesn't even know I exist on here, she thought.

Her phone suddenly dinged, showing a match. He had swiped back.

He sent the first message. *Hi,* it read.

Hey how are u? she responded.

I'm okay, my friends told me I should get on this and that it works, he said.

Oh! That's so funny lol. Where are you from?

Australia, I'm here studying abroad for the semester.

She paused. She wasn't sure if she should continue. She wanted a long term friend, not someone temporary. Before she could finish that thought, he sent another message.

I know it's a deal breaker here, but I'm hoping to come back. I love New York City, I want to be here long term.

The wine had drained out by this point and she stood frozen, unsure how to proceed. Something told her she shouldn't go for him, she'd get hurt. But she remembered all the Bollywood movies she'd watch with her family when she was younger. The main characters always found a way despite every obstacle, their feelings remaining true. She thought about how she had no plans tomorrow. Something deep down told her to go for it. One more friend couldn't hurt, she had to live in the moment. So she let her guard down.

They talked all night. They talked about what they wanted for themselves and their lives; their families, their favorite TV shows on Netflix. It was like she met her long lost best friend, and she knew he felt the same way.

Then they got to culture.

What part of India are you from? she asked.

My parents are from South India, I'm Christian.

She inhaled deeply.

She was well aware of the taboos that lay in India. The caste system shaped morals that consumed Indian households. The rule was: if they weren't like us, then you couldn't be with them. "Like us" meant anything like their family. Even though she was Hindu and he was Christian, their futures were still different. Chances were his family would want him to be with a Christian woman, from their part of India.

It might seem too Romeo and Juliet to understand, but history runs deep between the two cultures that were once one. After the Caribbean was colonized, Indians were brought as indentured laborers to work on sugar cane plantations. Since they were considered slaves, or of the lowest caste, they were looked down upon by the majority of Indian society, even decades after indenture ended. She knew her history and wasn't sure how he'd feel about it.

I thought you were Spanish, he said.

She rolled her eyes, but with a slight smile while she typed away. This was a common misconception among Caribbean people. Her light skinned complexion, and caramel toned hair always tended to confuse people.

No. My parents are from the Caribbean, but we're Hindus, she admitted. The façade was over. He was never going to talk to her again.

Oh that's cool. I actually have a lot of friends like you.

Her eyes lit up and she grinned from cheek to cheek. They talked all night for the next week. They talked about all angles of their lives, their hopes and dreams. She talked to him while at school and when she got home. At last, they decided to meet...

...Which is where she was running off to. They decided to meet at Grand Central Station, one of New York's most romantic destinations and a love symbol for most Bollywood movies. Ultimately, Grand Central was just the most convenient place for both of them. After frantically waiting on the fourth train to take her there, she finally made it.

Here, she messaged him. They had decided to meet at noon and it was 11:58.

She walked around the terminal nervously.

What if he's a crazy person? What if he'll kill me?

All these crazy thoughts ran through her head. Her mom knew where she was going to be, she had her location on her phone. But there was no response from him yet. As the time passed noon, she strolled into a stationary shop so people wouldn't think she was crazy walking around by herself. It was now 12:15.

"He isn't coming," she said as left the store.

Then someone tapped her shoulder. Her blood rushed as she turned around and looked up. He stood there, tall, dark and handsome, smiling from ear to ear. It was like the scene in *Khabi Khushie Khabi Gham* where Shah Rukh Khan walks in after being late to his family's Diwali celebration.

"You thought I wasn't coming didn't you?" he said, his accent strong.

She laughed. "I was just going to get some air."

He hugged her. "It's so nice to meet you finally."

"Yeah you too! I'm really excited. Where do you want to go today? You're the foreigner, so I'll show you around"

"I've already got that settled. We're going to the top of the Empire State Building. I paid for the VIP tour."

She was in shock. "What? Are you sure? How much do I owe you?"

"Don't worry about that. We're on a date."

It was too good to be true. Handsome and a gentleman.

That day was one of the best days of her life. It was a picture perfect date, like ones you see in movies. They went to the top of the Empire State Building and saw the amazing skyline of Manhattan. That was followed by drinks at a trendy bar in Soho, and then a romantic dinner in Little Italy. At the end of the day, he took her home. It was dark outside but the city was bright with its people and its lights. As he walked her to the steps, holding her hand, he stopped.

"I hope we can do this again," he told her. " I had a lot of fun with you."

"Yeah, I'd really like that... But you're going back to Australia." She knew this was only temporary.

He sighed. "I know, but I just felt this spark the whole time we were together today. I want to see where this goes."

They stood quiet for a moment. She looked down and he could tell she was nervous.

"Would your parents be okay with this?" she finally asked. "I don't want to invest my time if you can't be with me."

He knew what she meant, she didn't have to say more.

"Yes. They just want me to be happy."

She trusted his words and went in to hug him. As she moved closer, he lowered himself so he could kiss her. The city became even brighter.

They continued to see each other and the talking never stopped. They talked every day and never ran out of things to talk about. As Christmas approached, he had to go home since his visa was expiring. He told her he'd be back to be with her. They were falling in love and starting to see a future together. They were young, but the feeling was indescribable. She saw him off at the airport. She gave him a Christmas present and he did the same. She got him an Empire State building keychain to commemorate their first date. He bought her favorite chocolates.

They said their goodbyes and he promised her that he would be back. She told him to let her know when he was home. They kissed and went their separate ways.

***

It had been three months since he left. They still talked every day, but this time it was different. They weren't talking as much and she noticed he would take a longer time than usual to answer her. He also avoided her calls. She was a smart girl. She knew feelings don't go away that easily. She knew what was going on. She told him she loved him every day, but he had stopped saying it after a while, raising her anxiety.

She decided to ask him the question she was dreading.

"What's going on?" she blurted over the phone.

"What do you mean?" he responded.

"It's not the same. Things are different," she answered.

He knew, she knew. After a long pause he decided to say it.

"I told them. They aren't okay with it," he choked out the words.

She fought back tears and hung up the phone. She couldn't blame him. At the end of the day, that was his family and knowing how much she loved her own, she wouldn't risk losing them for anything. That was how he felt about his own too.

Love will find a way, she told herself. It always does.

Jumbie Queen

Alexandra Daignault

"jumbie |ˈjəmbē|

Noun W. Indian

a spirit of a (...) person, typically an evil one."

- Dictionary, Apple Inc.

Jumbie is the inherited pain of the whiteman's whip-

legacies of distortion, extensive scars.

Jumbie is our trauma.

Jumbie is our

inherited

pain.

Words fizz in my gut. I choke on them as they rise like yeast, snagging at my sternum. Each word heats up a tiny, angry, iron pressing itself into bone and tissue. I cannot cry. I know why I'm here.

Miss Becker looks at me, lines creasing her face like a well-loved, big-font, easy-to-read book.

"Do you want to tell me how you got those bruises, Billy?"

As she speaks, she reaches for my shadow-shimmered arms. I know why I'm here. I know why she has to ask me.

'Has to' bangs around in my head for a long time.

We have done this talk before, hopscotching between our words. I cannot tell her. The truth, although infinitely too much, seems much safer than the unknown that waits for big-small mixed-race brown girls.

I tell her what I can, "nightmares." We have had this talk before.

"Tell me about these nightmares." Her words skid across her desk, dipping easily into my chamomile tea before forcing themselves down my throat.

This is new, "I have two." I wonder if Mom would count this as a broken promise? Or if dreams are just dreams?

"What are they about Billy?" Her eyes are soft, but my name commands, warped by the twists of white lips.

"I dream about angels, Ma'am."

"Angels?"

I've disappointed her again. "Yes, Ma'am."

"You have nightmares about angels?"

Her eyes ask me a different question: *Are you being truthful?* I imagine large and wingless fragments, taking inspiration from Nanny's prized cabinet filled with beautiful white bone china.

"They haven't got wings," I shrug. As I speak, wide white whispers rise in eddies from the chalkboard. Word jumbies luminous through the rays of our class suncatchers.

"And they give you bruises?" she persists.

"They don't mean to." I shake my head to show the eyeless beings that I won't betray their secrets, dare not call them by their names.

"They are just so large, and so sad, that sometimes they forget to be gentlemen."

"The bruises look like they really hurt," her eyes trace the edges. She has no way of knowing. She cannot see the pink and newly purpled velvet of my vagina. If she could, then what?

Do not tell. My half-dream jumbie angels turn sightless chilling eyes on me. Just like that, I have missed the moment. I waited too long to answer Miss Becker's question.

"They don't sound like angels to me," she says. Nanny says in this country jumbies and angels are pretty much the same thing, the flip side of a coin. The bell rings and I can go back to my desk. Students filter in, snow boots caked with winter mud, mittens soaked in snot. I slip towards the bathroom, securing myself in a stall.

All the words I cannot say pour out of me, a final bile filled burp racking my ribs. She knows. She knows. Now what?

On my way back to the classroom, I see Sonny. His hands are deep in his pockets, shoulders hunched. We have no winter jackets. He offers me a smile, never quite reaching his almost-vacant eyes, a wingless jumbie angel in the flesh. As we pass, he catches my arm, whispering "Rani." Our secret word, heavy with ominous promise, meaning Queen. I shudder with revulsion, fear, shame...and love?

I almost turned to tell him, *I saw your live-dead soul in class today.* But, I do not. I suspect this specter haunts him just as much as me. My brother-cousin, a smushed up word encompassing and complicating what he means to me. What would Miss Becker say?

***

The ache in my trachea never really goes away, serving as a reminder. With each breath, it presses then expands, sending tiny tentacles of rot into my lungs. The doctor says I have asthma, that Dad should really stop smoking.

Dad responds with, "I should lay him at the bottom of the river." As I lie in bed, I play with the ache; breathing deeply, breathing lightly, counting and contracting. Once I read about the witching hour, where spirits come out to play. For me, Jumbie announces his arrival through the slither of the sliding door, when the house is still for hours.

Tonight will not be the night though. Dad didn't come home in the rusty red jeep for dinner. On these nights, Mom lies on the couch for hours. Sometimes I think she is sleeping with her green eyes open. Really though, she is preparing for battle.

I creep out of my bed, slipping soundless to the stairs. Through the bannister I can see the front door clearly. Mom has used a kitchen chair to jam the door knob, delaying the inevitable. The shoes from our welcome mat are strewn across the floor; and our red window scraper stands at the ready.

From the kitchen, I hear the repeat strum of Johnny Cash:

God's Gonna Cut You Down

If only, I think to myself. The brass knob rattles. *Jumbie.* Thirty seconds, and he knows the reason why the door won't open. His shout is slurred. Tomorrow we will have to answer the questions of the cul-du-sac.

"Fucking whore! You fucking dirty white-trash tramp." His words grow louder as he pushes, pulls, and works the door. Soon, Sonny is beside me. Right now, he is just my cousin. At this moment, I am safe with the lesser jumbie.

"I'm going to kill you!" His voice is getting louder.

I know it won't be long now. Animated by alcohol, my small and sweaty jumbie father, eyes like shiny rolling marbles, lurches into the light. The scraper makes stinging, slashing contact. A dangerous stillness falls; and I am running for the cordless hallway phone. I cannot escape his sounds, and the almost louder absence of her voice.

"You think you're tough now, do you?" His voice is rancid and full of hate. I hear the thud of her body making contact with the wall again and again. I'm racing back to my perch. At what point do I call? She is not screaming. We know it does not help. Tomorrow she will make him eggs, satiating the spirit, Jumbie, as it slips into slumber. Waiting.

This time though is different, he picks up the scraper, then she screams. I'm frozen as it echoes in my head. Sonny is snatching the phone from my grasp. Her hands are up over her head as she slumps against the wall. Relentlessly he beats her, until in a final burst of rage, he grabs her neck.

God's Gonna Cut You Down.

***

Distantly, Sonny speaks into the phone. It doesn't matter now. I'm running down the stairs. My fist connects with the fleshy bulge of his neck.

"STOP!"

My tears blind me as the slap sends me reeling towards Mom. I try to cover her with my body, protecting as best I can.

"You think you be a big girl?" his voice mocks.

He kicks me. I'm somewhere else. White-eyed luminous jumbies rise, coming for me and sucking up my hollow screams.

***

Blue lights illuminate, shimmering across white flesh. The policeman bends over me. His hot breath is sticky. What did he eat for dinner? I think about the red pulp of my insides, tomato choka mashed with care. The tile is cool against my cheek, I could sleep.

"You know though Frank," policeman number one whispers. "Those Brown people, they're not like us."

I fade into the floor, becoming his nothing, blue-grey cigarette ash caught in the wind.

***

Roti rolls in hot oil, expanding with delicious warmth. Nanny's arms are bespeckled with burns from this same chore, translucent glimmers on brown skin. Maybe Jumbies are satiated by the smell of hot chicken curry and dhaal puri, relegated to the corners of the room. Perhaps they are fearful of large Brown warrior women, equipped with wooden spoons and smarting smacks. I have slept well.

I think back to the social worker enunciating each letter: "Bil-ly. Am I saying it right?" She snaps her gum, spit conglomerating.

"Mhm," is the measured response. I am just another Brown face in the Children's Crisis Program.

"Oh wow! It's just like English!"

My face burns at the good intention in her eyes. Jumbie whispers, *villain.* Little does she know, little she does know.

"It is English!" Nanny has had enough of this woman, with her shiny shellacked nails, and too red mouth.

"Oh," her face falls, "I thought it might have been Hindi. That's what you speak back home, right? It's your first language?"

I focus my eyes, zoom in and away. *Big, Brown Nanny, the world's best granny,* stenciled in careful pencil across a pristine page. It's stark on the humming refrigerator.

Nan's hand extends to her hip. "This one," jutting her chin towards me, "she be born here, you fool." She steups loudly. Sonny snickers. The visit ends and all the paperwork is signed away. Two days in a group home, and now we are here; backpacks full of stories, folded between pairs of socks and days of the week underwear.

Now, it is just Nan and I in the kitchen; same-same, two peas in a pod, bedecked in our Walmart refinery. Soft blue sweatpants slide seamlessly into knitted green and purple slippers.

"Sonny." her voice rises as she calls, "you lazy ting!"

He climbs the stairs from the bowels of the house, already refusing.

"You so dark," Nan's brow furrows, "just like your father."

She spoons rice into plastic bowls, the white willow china saved for best.

"Eat," a firm command. "You both so thin-thin."

On the third helping, Sonny slows. His hands are sweaty, I cannot meet his eyes.

"Take more chicken," Nan tells him, ladling green-green curry into his bowl.

I can feel him asking for an alliance. I cannot meet his eyes, cramming my mouth with our soft rice.

"You gon waste this food?" Her voice hardens. "Your parents send you all t'way up here for better life, and what you do? You waste it? Your uncle, by the time he was twelve...eh... you balling your fists at me? I give you the licken of you life, you hear?"

Like lightning, her soap soaked spoon slices through the air.

"Lazy!" Smack. "Stupid!" Smack.

Sonny's hands defend his head.

Jumbie rises, reflected in the tiny rainbow bubbles settling in the sink, hungry once again. He turns his vacant eyes on me. I will pay the price tonight, the cost of silence.

***

I lie in the spare bedroom full of things I'm sure no one's Nanny needs. Long, yellowed, Island photographs in mismatched frames trace a lineage of serious gold eyes and gaunt hunger, even in black and white. Sonny's father and my dad stark in front of a wooden verandah, white shirts billowing. Brothers.

Nan, smelling faintly of Limacol, rubs coconut oil into my still there bruises.

"I love all my grandchildren like the fingers on my hand," her voice is layered with the weight of us. "But you girl, you be like my thumb, I just couldn't do without."

I have never been anyone's favourite, an expensive space to occupy.

"So pale," her words trickle, condensation dripping down my neck.

When Nan leaves, I wonder how we ended up here, in wide white prairies, wearing winter as if it's timeless. I want to call her back and ask, *was it always this way?*

As the night deepens, I keep the lamp on, sending cascades of fragmented brilliance across the room. I am waiting. The witching hour starts with the creak of a well-used stair. *Jumbie's coming.* The silence stretches around his steps. I want to run. Instead, I pull the white and floral sheet over my head. I know why he's here. Sonny opens the door.

Just Be Yourself
Natasha Persaud

This morning was fourteen-year-old Anissa's first day at a new school. She was nervous and excited.

"Anissa, come and eat yuh breakfast," her mom shouted. Her Guyanese accent boomed from the bottom of the stairs.

"Coming mommy!" Anissa grabbed her backpack and rushed downstairs.

Her mother made fresh baigan choka, roti and hot tea. The eggplant, mushed with seasoning and spices, mixed with Indian style bread was a popular dish in her parent's home country, Guyana. In a way, it was Guyana's version of scrambled eggs and bread.

"Anissa, hurry up and eat, yuh don't want to be late."

Anissa quickly finished half of her food and left with her older brothers for school.

"Dis gyal always leaving back she food!" her mother exclaimed as she left.

Anissa and her two older brothers arrived at school. As she walked through the school she read her schedule to herself. She spotted a Brown girl down the hallway. Anissa was excited to see someone else who looked like her. Although she dressed differently; she wore ripped jeans, a crop top, and had long, straight hair.

"Hey! I'm new. My name is Anissa," she eagerly said.

"You must be lost," the pretty Brown girl said rudely and laughed.

She turned her back to Anissa and joined a group of girls and guys laughing. Her group of friends dressed just like her. Some looked older, but Anissa couldn't tell how much older. As she quietly walked away, she could feel the group staring at her.

As Anissa entered her first class, another Brown girl smiled as she walked past her. Slowly but surely, she made it through each of her classes. Finally, it was time for Gym. Anissa loved sports since her dad and brothers were huge sports fans. She was excited to move her body after sitting all day. Little did she know, none of the other girls liked playing sports. When it was time to play, all the girls sat on the bench, talking and joking with each other.

"You've got to be kidding me!" she heard one girl say.

Anissa walked over to the girls, trying to make friends again.

"Hey guys, what's up? I'm Anissa, the new girl."

Even with that introduction, the girls just looked at her.

"Go away loser. We're not interested in being friends," one of the girls said.

Anissa didn't realize it was the same girl from earlier. She frowned and walked away from the group. As gym class came to an end, she watched as the other girls put on makeup and checked themselves out in the mirror. They were all talking about a party that was coming up. A party Anissa knew she wouldn't be invited to.

***

It was finally lunchtime; what Anissa thought was going to be a great day, was the complete opposite. Everyone sat in groups, but Anissa, groupless, had to sit alone. She took out the chicken chow mein her mom had packed her.

"What is that? It looks like worms!" someone from across the table exclaimed.

"It's food from my culture, why would I eat worms?" Anissa proudly said back.

She saw her brothers; they were also in groups. Brian, who was in eleventh grade, hung out with the same kids she said hi to this morning. She definitely didn't want to try and talk to him while he was with his friends. Her other brother Nathan, who was in twelfth grade, was talking with a few guys and the girl who had smiled at her that morning. She grabbed her lunch and walked over to her brother in hopes she could sit with him.

"Hey Nissa, how's your day going? Want to sit with us?" Nathan asked.

"My day's going horrible. I haven't made any friends yet," Anissa said angrily.

Everyone looked sad when they heard that.

"I'm sorry to hear your day isn't going well, would you like to talk about it? I'm Alana by the way. No girl, or anyone really, should feel that way. I can be your friend."

Anissa told Alana about her day.

"You shouldn't feel bad, that was brave of you. It shows your confidence."

Alana briefly told her about the blog that she ran. "It's run by regular Brown girls like us. One of the highlights shows how strong we can be and why we should never give up. Check it out when you get a chance."

RING

The school bell rang and everyone had five minutes to get to class.

"It was nice meeting you!" Anissa and Alana said to each other.

Anissa waited outside of her class, ready to start. While she was waiting, some of the popular kids she ran into earlier passed by, staring at her. Anissa didn't even want to look past them anymore, she just anxiously waited for the teacher.

"Oh, hello," an older woman said.

As she went to open the door, her books fell out of her grip, landing on the floor. Anissa helped the teacher pick up her items and they both went into the classroom and placed everything down.

"Thank you dear, you must be the new student...A-Anca?"

"Anissa, miss." Teachers were always mispronouncing Anissa's name. *It can't be that hard to pronounce*, she thought to herself.

"Oh, terribly sorry hun. You'll have to correct me if I make that mistake again. Welcome to my art class! You came at a great time, today we're starting a new visual project about what you like about yourself. Why don't you find a seat Alisha."

"It's Anissa, miss."

A-ni-ssa, she sounded it out in her head, getting annoyed.

Anissa found her seat in the front. Minutes had now passed, and the teacher introduced her to the class and explained their new project. Everyone was nice so far. Anissa was finally feeling good about her day, until the group of girls from her gym class showed up. Their eyes were red, and they smelled like a skunk.

Oh great... Please don't be in this class, Anissa thought. Her teacher was frustrated as well.

"Samantha and Tamia! You're half an hour late again. Did you girls get a late slip?"

"Chill out Miss S," the girl Anissa had said hi too said.

"I don't think you girls realize how rude and disruptive you are being. I hope you weren't doing what I think you were doing."

"Miss S, that's really none of your business," Tamia said.

Miss S shook her head as the two girls found their seat in the back. Anissa watched as they put their feet up on the table and pulled out their phones. *Thank god they didn't see me*, she thought, watching her teacher leave the room.

"Oh my gosh Tamia, isn't that the loser that tried being our friend?" Anissa heard Samantha practically yell across the room.

Ugh too late.

Tamia laughed. "Oh my gosh, it is! As if we'd ever be her friend."

They had only been in the class for a few minutes when they both pulled out snacks to eat. *We just had lunch*, Anissa thought. Miss S came back into the room and her frustration with Tamia and Samantha hadn't seized.

"Girls, that's it! I've tolerated enough from you two. You know the rules, and you two have been completely disrespectful towards the class and I. I'm calling the principal and you can answer to him."

Within a few minutes, the principal came down and escorted the girls out.

The day finally came to an end and Anissa waited at the school entrance for her brothers. Brian walked down the hallway with some of the guys he hung out with at lunch.

"Later man, I'll see you this weekend!"

They gave props to each other and went their separate ways. The guys stared at Anissa as they walked past her, making her feel uncomfortable for a moment. She spotted Nathan laughing and walking down the hallway with Alana. He was always making someone laugh.

"Oh hey, Anissa! How was the rest of your day?" Alana asked.

"Hey! It was alright," Anissa grumbled the last part.

"It'll get better hun," Alana looked at her reassuringly.

"Hun? What are you, an old lady?" Nathan joked.

"Ugh, you're so rude!" Alana joked back. "I've got to go. Don't forget to look up the BGD blog, Anissa."

"What does BGD mean?" Nathan asked.

"Brown Girl Diary," Anissa and Alana both said.

"You put your diary out on the web?" Nathan laughed.

"No, not like that, it's a blog made to bring confi—"

"Are there games on it? Answers to our test? Funny videos?" Nathan asked, cutting her off.

"No, there are articles," Alana said, frustrated with Nathan's comments.

"Oh, boring! We gotta go! Later, Grandma!"

Finally in the comfort of her home, Anissa thought about Samantha and Tamia, wondering what had happened to them in the office. She shrugged it off, showered, and ate a fresh tennis roll with cheese. She loved the hint of sweetness and fluffiness of the bun. It was one of her favourite snacks. She sat in her room trying to focus on her work, but ended up wandering off to the Brown Girl Diary blog Alana had told her about.

"Whoah, there's so much stuff here," Anissa said to herself. She became fascinated with everything she was learning, not even noticing when her dad came home from work. When she looked at the time, it was after 1 in the morning.

"I should go sleep," she yawned.

***

Over the next few weeks, the talk around school had been about an upcoming party. Anissa wished she had gotten to go, but was glad she didn't. Brian had got home after 2 a.m. and their parents were not happy at all. There was talk about people drinking and smoking and Anissa couldn't imagine how much trouble she would have gotten into if she had gone with her brother. She also heard that Samantha and Tamia had gotten suspended for three weeks following the art class incident.

When Alana wasn't busy, she spent almost every lunch with Anissa. Walking into class, Anissa heard more about the party.

"Did you see what they were wearing? And how pretty they looked?"

"Yeah, their makeup was so pretty and their hair too! But did you see someone wearing an ugly sweater today? It's bigger than their body."

"Ugh, they looked ridiculous."

Suddenly, Anissa started to feel bothered again. *Were they talking about me?* she thought. She knew her sweater was bigger than her body, and that she never wore makeup. But her hair wasn't crazy, it was curly. Anissa asked to be excused and ran to the bathroom. Looking in the mirror, tears started coming to her eyes. *They were talking about me.*

As she started to cry, the door swung open, but Anissa didn't bother to look up.

"Anissa, what happened?" It was Alana.

"Everyone was so mean to me, they made fun of me," Anissa sniffed. She told her that they made fun of her clothes and how it made her feel.

"That's horrible. You know whatever they're saying is not true right? Remember on the blog, how it talks about why we should be proud of who we are? Our ancestors went through a lot, they've been through hell and back. Everyone is created differently and beautifully. Everyone has something unique about them. Your clothes don't define you. It's what's inside that shines brighter than you'll ever see. Your family came to this country for a better life. Brian told me that you guys used to help out on your grandma's farm when you were little. You're a lot braver than you think. There are many girls who struggle and feel like they're alone, but the truth is we're not. I want you to believe in that Nissa."

"Wow Lana, you're right. I've been so caught up in fitting in and making friends. I've always had this idea of high school being full of laughs, friends, boys. You know, like on TV. I haven't thought about Guyana in ages, let alone what my ancestors might have gone through. I shouldn't let a few people's opinions get in my way. Thank you." Anissa dried her eyes, her head clearer than ever.

***

"I am proud to say these are the things I like about myself thanks to the Brown Girl Diary blog and my new friend Alana. An important message I was taught was to love yuhself, nourish, and grow. Claim yuh space, and be true to you.

Stigmas doh exist no more. Remember wheh yuh come from, but take pride in weh yuh going. Change the narrative and make it yours. You is the Nexx Genn Coolie Gyal. Reclaim it, embrace it and add slight peppah."

As Anissa finished her visual presentation, everyone clapped for her.

"Amazing job Anissa! Learning to love yourself is definitely a process."

Karela
Anna Maria Chowthi

Hardeo stood straight-backed and unmoving, his palms sweaty and his heart racing. He was waiting in line at Cheddi Jagan International Airport with two fake passports in one hand and his three-year-old daughter Salisha in the other. He just had to pass through security in Guyana, and he would be fine.

When it was his turn, the security officer took the two fake passports and checked them thoroughly before giving them back to Hardeo.

"Go ahead," the officer said.

Hardeo murmured a quick 'thank you' as he walked away. Only when he was out of the security station's sight did he allow himself to breathe a sigh of relief.

Hardeo boarded the plane with Salisha at his side. He felt a wave of lightness wash over him. The hardest part was over and he was looking forward to reuniting with his wife when they arrived in Toronto, Ontario.

They landed in Toronto seven hours later on a frigid cold evening in December. Heading off the plane with a single carry-on, they entered the customs line. This was the other difficult part, but at least he'd already made it into Canada. He waited in line until it was his turn. When the officer signalled him to come forward and asked for his passports, Hardeo knew this was it.

He handed over the passports to the officer. When the officer said the fake names, Leonard and Katherine, he gave a quick 'yes.'

"These passports look fake," the officer said.

"I'd like to apply for refugee status in the country of Canada," Hardeo told him.

***

Salisha was on her way home with her friend Candice. The girls had walked home together every day after school since they were six. Her stomach was already growling; she was always hungry by the time school was over and as soon as she got home, the first thing she always did was eat. Her parents cooked meals daily, a routine they continued even after moving from Guyana, although they both had full-time jobs. A routine, Salisha acknowledged wryly to herself, that she regularly underappreciated. The truth was, she loved her parents' cooking. There were only a few dishes she didn't really care for. Overall, the food was one of the best parts of growing up West Indian.

She walked through the front door, quickly kicking her shoes off into the corner, and went straight to the large pot warming on the kitchen stove. She opened it excitedly.

"Karela again?"

She wrinkled her nose in distaste and slammed the pot cover hard enough for the neighbors to hear. Hema had been observing her daughter from the moment she got in, anticipating this moment. She knew Salisha hated karela. She also knew her daughter was dramatic.

"There's bread you can eat," Hema said matter-of-factly.

"Man, you people only want to starve people in this house," Salisha sighed.

Dramatic, Hema thought, laughing in her mind. She knew Salisha would eat it regardless, but first she had to make a fuss.

Salisha reluctantly dished out some rice and the karela cooked with shrimp. Whenever she was forced to have it, she always wondered why anyone would eat such a vegetable. *Who thought of cooking this ugly thing*, she thought. Unfortunately for her, it was a staple in the Chawl household.

In her best moments, though, Salisha was becoming more grateful for her parents' consistency in the kitchen. Coming home to the spices of masala, curry powder and geera when her parents made curried dishes was her favourite; although it made her hair smell like curry until she washed it.

It didn't help that she had long, thick hair for the smell to latch on to. Her hair grew past her backside and was so heavy it gave her headaches. She wasn't allowed to cut it, though; although she'd been raised most of her life in Toronto, her parents still held onto many of their old ways from Guyana. Culturally, a girl's long hair was highly regarded as the ideal of beauty. Salisha found this annoying at times. She couldn't wait until she was old enough to cut it off. The headaches were bad enough, but Salisha hated how her long hair made her look even skinnier. She also questioned this obsession with the way girls had to look; from the ideal body type to the perfect skin complexion.

Salisha was skinny with caramel skin and a button nose. Her almond eyes sometimes looked Southeast Asian, confusing people about what country she could be from. When she opened her mouth, that confusion usually ended. Being a mouthy girl, she found it beneficial to hold on to her roots through language. Words like *skunt* and phrases like *meh nah able* were part of her regular lexicon. Her language and word choices made her feel connected to her Guyanese culture.

She often felt different from her peers and struggled with feeling not West Indian enough in certain social circles and not westernized enough in others. It was a complex she'd struggled with since she was young. And it wasn't like there was just one thing that she struggled with, like the way she was supposed to look, it was everything. Salisha was always consciously and subconsciously navigating friendships, relationships, Western systems, and home systems in ways she didn't always realize. She was constantly shaping who she was and who she wanted to be while figuring out how to embrace and hold onto her Guyanese culture at home and on the inside, while living in the Canadian world on the outside.

After dinner, Salisha usually spent time with her friends in the area. She'd meet up with Candice again and they would play sports (if the boys were out too) or walk around talking. It was a nice, cool summer evening and today the boys were outside. She enjoyed playing soccer in particular and she and Candice seemed to be the only girls that wanted to get in on the game. This was also why she and Candace got along so well. Salisha usually found it difficult to connect with other girls her age, especially Guyanese girls, apart from her cousin Nadia, who shared her passion for books.

She found it hard to hold a conversation with most girls, because they usually only talked about two things; complaining about their boyfriends or complaining about not having boyfriends.

Even though she wasn't fond of the relationship conversations her peers regularly had, Salisha did have a boyfriend of her own. Ryan was a dream in her eyes. She smiled to herself, thinking of him. He was tall with long hair and hazel eyes. They were the same age, but went to different high schools in the city. They'd met through a mutual family friend when they were thirteen and had spent the night in their own corner talking about everything and nothing. They hadn't kept in touch afterwards and didn't see each other again for another two years.

This time, Ryan didn't let her go. He'd spent two years thinking about how different, smart, and real Salisha was. Since then, they spoke on the phone every night, spent weekends watching movies at Yorkdale Mall, and dreaming up dreams for their future.

Salisha was usually attracted to Guyanese boys, but the ones she'd met at school were usually less academic focused and too carefree for her liking. Luckily, she and Ryan seemed to work. His intellect was attractive, he was into the cosmos and quantum physics. They'd have great conversations at night about all sorts of things. Usually not what they learnt in school, but what they read on their own. They bonded over their love of learning, shared tastes in movies and food, going against the grain, and of course, culture.

After the soccer game, Salisha remembered she had to get home and finalize what she was going to wear the next day. She had her high school graduation ceremony and it was giving her mixed feelings. She was excited to graduate and go to university in September, but a part of her felt like she needed some breathing space. Her parents were on the verge of divorce and it was affecting many aspects of her life.

As she was lost in thought about her parents, her phone rang. It was her mom. She knew it was a phone call to remind her not to be out too late. Since she was nearly home, she ignored it.

When she got home, she said hi to her mom and went straight into her room.

"Make sure you come off the phone before your dad gets home!" her mom yelled as she ran up the stairs.

Salisha kissed her teeth. She and her dad didn't get along. He wasn't home because, as usual, he'd gone over to the house across the street to drink after he'd helped Hema cook dinner. Some nights he would come home so drunk, he would wake up the entire house stumbling over furniture. There were also other nights that were even worse. Those nights broke Salisha's spirit and tore her heart in two.

As Salisha was grabbing her phone to call Ryan, she started hearing the telltale noises that her father was home. She put down her phone, took a deep, steadying breath, and went downstairs.

"Yuh fucking bitch!" Salisha heard her dad say. "Meh know wah yuh a do! Meh buy dis fucking house and feed yuh pickney, and yuh nah get none thanks!"

"Go to bed, man," Hema said, trying to brush Hardeo off.

"Who yuh tink yuh a talk to. Come here!" Hardeo grabbed Hema's wrist.

Hema saw Salisha coming down the stairs.

"Go in your room, Salisha."

Hema was always trying to protect Salisha from the chaos that was her marriage with Hardeo.

"Let her go, Dad. Go to bed," Salisha said, walking towards her parents.

He turned back to Hema, "Yuh see how yuh teach this pickney to talk to me!" Salisha and Hema looked at each other, confused but not surprised.

"Dad, just go upstairs and sleep." She looked him in his eyes with no fear.

"Why yuh always on yuh mudda side? Yuh know what this woman put me through?" Hardeo's eyes were barely staying open.

"I'm not on anyone's side." She was definitely on her mom's side.

"You're a liar. Nobody does care about me in this house!" Hardeo said. His voice was full of drunken emotion, as he made his way up the staircase and into his room.

Salisha was relieved. Tonight was one of the good nights. There were nights that were so bad, she had to tear her dad away from her mom. Her parents often got into physical and verbal fights about drinking and money, and Salisha usually had to intervene, lest the situation escalate.

Wearily, she went back to her room. As she was passing her mom, she stopped.

"How much longer are we going to do this for Mom?"

They stared at each other in silence. Salisha shook her head in disappointment, went into her room, locked the door, and sat on her bed. As she started to think about the nights that didn't end up this forgiving, her eyes welled up with water. She shook her head and wiped away her tears. She didn't have time for this, she had to sort out what she was wearing tomorrow and give Ryan a call.

She took deep breaths, picked up her cell phone, and dialed Ryan's number.

"Hey babe, how was your day? Dad's drunk again."

***

The next day, after a half day of classes, Salisha and all her friends were excited to get home and get ready for their graduation ceremony. She was looking forward to celebrating, and when she got a text from Ryan asking if they'd have any alone time after the ceremony, she was thrilled. She told him they could hang out after the ceremony and do whatever he wanted.

When Salisha got home, she ate chicken curry with rice, showered, and did her makeup and hair. She was ready to go.

Hema drove the family to Salisha's graduation ceremony. During the drive, she was thinking about what a milestone this was for her daughter and how different it was for girls to grow up in Canada compared to her experience in Guyana. Many times, she felt like she didn't know how to properly raise Salisha in Canada. All she knew was that she was glad she'd done it.

Salisha was sitting in the front of the school theatre with her classmates, fully appreciating the moment. There were performances, awards and speeches. During her principal's speech, he said, *you made it*, and that hit home. Tears came down her face as she thought about it. But it was the moment her name was called, that it really hit her. As she received her certificate and walked across the stage, it dawned on her what a privilege this was and how hard she'd worked to get to this point.

After the ceremony, Salisha said bye to her parents and hung out with her friends outside the school while she waited for Ryan. Ryan was going to meet her after his ceremony, which happened to be on the same day. She was looking forward to their quality time. When Ryan arrived, he greeted Salisha and her friends. The couple hung around for a couple minutes before going their own way.

As they were leaving, Ryan grabbed Salisha's hand. "I have a surprise for you!"

"Really? You didn't have to. I didn't get you anything!" Salisha said, now feeling guilty.

"No, don't worry about that. It's more for the both of us," he assured her.

"Okay, I'm excited." Salisha was looking forward to what Ryan had planned.

The surprise was at Ryan's house, so they grabbed a cab and headed to the apartment he lived in with his mom.

When they arrived, Ryan took Salisha to his room. In the room, there was a large balloon with 'Congratulations' written in big letters. There were also several white balloons floating around.

"Wow, Ryan, this is amazing." Salisha was caught off guard.

He held her hand and took her to the bed.

"So, I did this for a reason, not just because we graduated," Ryan started to explain.

"Uh huh," Salisha was waiting to see where this was going.

"I know that you've been having a hard time at home. Things have been tough for you and I wanted to do something about that."

As he was explaining, Ryan got up, picked up some strips of paper, and two pens.

"Let's mark today as a new chapter. We're going to write some wishes and goals on here, attach them to the balloons, and release them from the balcony. Let's put these dreams in the cosmos, babe."

Salisha was speechless at first. Who even thought of things like this in real life? She was grateful to have him and immediately started thinking about what she would write.

"I just wanna be the best person I can be," she started to say to Ryan. "You know, I've struggled a lot with fitting in and everything I've got going on at home. I'm tired of the expectations, but I don't think I can change that. So, I just want to be the best me."

Ryan nodded. Of course Salisha had a simple answer to what could otherwise be a complicated thing to think about. They wrote their dreams, hopes and wishes down, attached them to the balloons and released them into the cosmos for the universe to answer.

***

Sonia was rummaging through drawers looking for the earrings she had bought for tonight's graduation ceremony. She sighed, unable to find the ones she was looking for. She decided to borrow something from her mom.

She went into her parents room and began digging through the drawers. When she opened one of them, she saw a box with her name on it. It was obvious it was a graduation gift from her parents. She opened it, and inside was a handwritten book. As she flipped through the pages, she realized it was a recipe book, with more than fifty recipes of traditional Guyanese dishes. She was in awe. She loved Guyanese food, it was one of the only things that made her feel cultured and represented her caramel skin. As she was flipping through, she was glad to see her mom still cooked many of these dishes, until she saw karela with shrimp. What was that? After going through the book, she decided to call her mom.

The phone rang and went to voicemail.

"Hi, you've reached Salisha at...."

Sonia hung up and called her dad.

"Hi, you've reached Ryan at..."

Sonia hung up and texted in the family group chat. *Mom, Dad, I found the recipe book. So cool! What's karela?*

Neither Here Nor There

Savita Prasad

"Are we 'other'?" Henna asked.

We shared a silent perplexed look before quietly returning our eyes to the paper laying on the table in front of us. Releasing a frustrated puff of air, my fingers mindlessly traced the raised black ink on the paper.

Warmth was radiating off of the body sitting next to me.

"We're Asian, right?" Nick was leaning in too close for my comfort.

My skin was scorching from the contact. Trying to resist the fluttering sensation and the lightheadedness stirred by the soft whisper in my ear, I coolly replied he was indeed Asian.

I picked up the paper and studied the printed choices on the sheet. White, Black/African American, Asian, American Indian/ Alaska Native, Native Hawaiian/ Other Pacific Islander, Hispanic/ Latino, and Other.

I was born in the borough of Queens in the state of New York. My parents and best friend Henna were born and raised in Guyana. Despite eighteen revolutions around the golden sun, I didn't know how to define my race/ethnicity. On the hindlegs of the sturdy wooden chair, I swayed back and forth.

When we met, Nick assumed I was Indian. I didn't correct him. I could easily blend in with my olive skin tone, almond-shaped eyes, prominent nose, and long raven hair. I have a common Indian surname, Prasad. I am also 95% certain my great-grandparents are Indian. Checking the Asian box on the survey would not be downright wrong since I am part of the Indian diaspora. Yet, as I sat there, I felt like I was not disclosing the entire truth.

Growing up, I thought I was Indian. I loved my Indian heritage. I inherited my parents' love for Bollywood songs and movies even though no one could grasp the language. We used Bollywood movies as a life jacket, keeping ourselves afloat so we could swim back to our roots. Between twirling like the heroines in the long, vibrantly colored movies, to dressing up in a lehenga accompanied by a silky glittering dupatta draped over my shoulder with a colorful bindi to match on my forehead, I yearned to connect to my ancestors.

India is a huge country with global acknowledgment. Pride used to flow through my blood knowing I was from Indian descent. I claimed the country and the accomplishments of its people as my own. Trivial facts such as India winning the pageant titles Miss Universe, Miss World, and Miss Asia Pacific in the year 2000 made me feel like I won and was just as beautiful as the Indian women who won. Wisecracks about the stereotypical Indian careers in medicine, engineering, and technology made me feel like I was capable and smart. When someone made the incorrect assumption that I was Indian, I went along with it because it made me feel worthy.

But I knew I wasn't really Indian. I didn't realize this until high school, after interacting with kids whose parents came directly from India.

When I was fourteen years old, I was swept off my feet by a boy who was smart, funny, humble, and genuinely kind. I relished in joy when he tilted his head back and a contagious belly laugh would erupt from him, echoing across the room. My entire body warmed under his gaze and hummed whenever he was too close. He made me feel safe. We burned the midnight light over the phone for three years, mapping out our futures together.

On the night his parents found out about us, my heart shattered when he told me they wanted us to terminate the relationship. They didn't have any interest in meeting me or getting to know who I was. While he was talking at a hundred miles per hour, constructing the necessary steps to keep our relationship alive and secret, I struggled to wrap my head around what was happening.

I wasn't sure what his parents didn't like. I am a good person. I was at the top of my class; well behaved, and treated everyone with respect. I wanted to become a doctor. I had plans for improving our community. I would have understood if their concern was about us being in love at a young age, but I knew that wasn't the issue. After some coercion, he admitted his parents wanted him to marry and settle down with a nice Punjabi girl in the future. In other words, someone who was authentically Indian. I didn't fit their image because I was Coolie.

That phone call changed everything between us. We couldn't look each other in the eye following that night. An awkward silence and distance were maintained until we graduated. With the snap of my fingers, the future we planned on building had vanished. I was devastated.

I didn't understand what it meant to be Indian then, and I still don't know today. Was I not Indian because I wasn't considered Desi or because I didn't speak Hindi? Was it because my great-grandparents decided to put roots down in the Caribbean? (They didn't have a choice.) Was it because of my love for soca and chutney tunes? Or was it because I spoke a creolized version of English when I was at home? It was the first time I felt the sting from the whip of discrimination and the shame that followed it.

Clinging to the Indian culture in hopes of being accepted into their community to redeem my ancestors' parting from the motherland was shallow. Most Indians were unaware of the existence of Indians in the Caribbean. When I revealed to members of the South Asian Club that I didn't know what a *kulfi* or a *mango lassi* was, they looked at me like I was a purple alien with three bulging eyes on my forehead. I didn't understand the hype around a person being of Sindhi or Gujarati background. I may have looked Indian, but I didn't belong to the club, or the culture. The only thing I was certain of was that I was a fake Indian.

Graduating high school, I wanted to leave the bubble of suburban Queens and start a new chapter in college. In the bustling city of New York, meeting people with different backgrounds and finding commonalities between cultures and religions was thrilling. It felt like a new start. I felt light, like I could breathe again. I laughed when people confused Guyana with Ghana and excitedly explained the brief history of how Indians ended up in this tiny obscure country. But I quickly found out very few people were excited to learn more, most remained confused or indifferent.

"So you're Indian then."

"Not really..."

"But you look Indian."

"I know."

Automatically stamped and boxed in as Indian, looking away and staying quiet became the norm after responding to where I came from. Saying you were born in America was not a sufficient answer for people when you have features considered exotic. There wasn't any real visual representation in mainstream media to refer to. I didn't know how to respond when the rest of the world was telling me that I was Indian while simultaneously dealing with the Indian community's rejection. I was neither here nor there.

I peered over at Nick as he checked off 'Asian.' I would be lying if I said I wasn't interested. I was drawn by the way he took things apart and put them back together. He had a creative instinct. Nick's family was from the state of Gujarat. Henna and I, on the other hand, had no idea which part of India our ancestors were from. There were no written letters or narratives left behind to link our ancestors to the country. If there were an anecdote that wasn't destroyed, it wasn't in English. We didn't have the honor of knowing our family's history or the language they spoke. I didn't even know of my grandfather's name until a few weeks ago when I found his birth records hidden in my mom's dresser. The records show he was born into the indentured service in 1912 in Guyana. I can only infer that our ancestors were probably from a lower caste and were either kidnapped or tricked into boarding a packed ship that would take them across the world. There was shame associated with this relocation because indentured servants were the new slaves.

Distraught by the way my last relationship ended, I didn't feel worthy to engage with Nick. I turned my back on my Indian heritage in the last year. I lost interest in the world of Bollywood. I stopped singing Bollywood songs during long car rides. I stopped watching the King Khan movies I grew up with. I opted to wear elegant dresses over the traditional Indian attire at religious events. Subconsciously, I knew my background was different from South Asians' and I experienced the inferior complex that came with those feelings. I have never seen an Indian person at my mandir and I've never gone to an authentic Indian temple to pray, despite sharing the same religion. Growing up, I hardly saw the Desi and West Indian communities interact. In trying to assimilate into South Asian culture, I was disconnected from who I was. I poured myself into the Caribbean part of me, hoping to fill the gap of wanting to belong.

I was wrong.

Sometimes I pictured Guyana as a high school student struggling to find its place during lunchtime amongst various cliques in the cafeteria. Guyana's location is unique given the country is located on the North Atlantic coast of South America. When most people think of South America, the Spanish and Portuese languages often come to mind. However, this former British colony is the only country in South America where English is the official language, even though it is creolized. Unlike the other Caribbean countries, Guyana is not in the vicinity of the Caribbean Sea, nor is it an island. It's even been put up for debate whether Guyana belonged to the Caribbean community. Despite having a similar socio-historical background, I could see how our sister country, Trinidad and Tobago, was geographically considered a part of the Caribbean and how Guyana was not. Nevertheless, because the headquarters of CARICOM Seat of Secretariat is located in the capital Georgetown, Guyana was accepted as a key member of the Caribbean community. With similar trauma bonds as the other islands, I felt like I was finally going to be seen and accepted when I joined the Caribbean Club.

The Caribbean united the Afro and Indo diaspora under the term West Indians. We made connections over snacks like Bigfoot chips, Chubby's soda, Chico's gum, and Caramel Waffle bars along with foods such as doubles, cookup, and pepperpot. I had people to jump up and buss a wine with when I played dancehall or soca music. I didn't have to worry about being judged when my accent slipped or having to explain jokes like, "*yuh tek yuh eyes and pass meh.*" There was comfort in laughing over how our mothers would have supernatural dreams the night before a planned adventure, the jumbie stories our grandparents used to tell us when we were kids, and using Vick's or limacol for everything. Despite the connection, it still felt like something was missing. While most members of the club were open to playing with colorful powdered dyes during Phagwah and lighting diyas during Diwali, it still felt like I was denying a part of myself.

There were distinct differences in the history of how the African slaves and the Indian indentured servants came to the Caribbean. Though we came from a similar historical background of exploitation, we were not the same. There were certain privileges that came with being from East Indian descent. Indo-Caribbeans swept it under a rug and pretended the trauma didn't happen. No one talked about what it was like being a descendant of an indentured servant. Looking around the Caribbean Club, I saw that most members were Black and/or Latino, groups that were known to be oppressed in America. A part of me felt guilty being there. Culturally we were similar, but I didn't look like I fit in even if I sounded like I did. Again, I felt neither here nor there.

There were days I wondered if I was making a big deal about being excluded and boxed in, knowing that other groups had it worse. I had the privilege of blending in, staying quiet in different groups, and partaking in shared experiences. I knew I didn't fit in with any one particular group and there were times I felt invisible. I noticed the lack of Indo-Caribbean representation on campus, but I didn't know of any statistics.

I didn't feel Indian nor Caribbean enough. I may look Indian, but I didn't sound Indian. Growing up in a neighborhood known as "Little Guyana" in Richmond Hill, everyone knew of the foods you ate, the music you listened to, and shared the same cultural experiences. I was not aware I was part of a culture that was vastly different from America's mainstream until I branched out. Even the way we spoke English was different. I found my voice and strength in my community.

My parents fled Guyana after the country went into a political uproar. Their focus was to build a better life for themselves and our family in America. They had no desire to get involved in race or politics considering the corruption they escaped from. Despite Guyanese people making up the fifth largest foreign-born population in the city, without including people from other Caribbean countries with Indian ancestry, there seemed to be a lack of representation. Our population was lost in the double displacement.

As a curious kid, I tried to understand why my relatives did certain things and tried to understand their thought process for the rules they made. The explanations West Indians typically gave for frivolous matters involved superstitions and old-wives tales. For example, a person's short stature was explained if someone hopped over them. Yet, when it came to significant issues, my questions were dodged. I wanted to know why no one spoke Hindi or why my grandmother's wrist had a tattoo but she was adamant against the idea of her grandchildren getting one. I wanted to know which of my mom, aunt and uncles' physical features belonged to my grandfather and why my grandmother got married so young to a man nineteen years her senior. There was so much that I wanted to know, but they either couldn't, or wouldn't, give me the answers I was dying to hear. Their focus was on surviving and being content. They were tired and wanted the stories of their hardships to die with them. They were determined to give their children a good life.

There aren't many places I could go to for answers. In school we didn't learn of indentured servitude in the Caribbean. There aren't any museums featuring the artifacts of my ancestors. Our history was erased and the British treatment of my ancestors was excused. I don't understand what happened in the late 1830s or how it made sense to the British colonizers to treat people like they were less than human; stripping people of their identity, language, and culture. It is infuriating to know my ancestors were not able to leave behind an artifact or narrative to tell their story. I'm fuming for those who were able to complete their indentured service contract under inhumane conditions and had no way to return to their home in India. My blood boils for those who didn't realize how far away they were from their home and drowned trying to swim there. I am enraged for those who were whipped when speaking in their native tongue. I am disappointed because I know our culture is currently in danger of dying. I am angry because it is the 21st century and I am forced to check off a box that represents where my family came from. There is no box I can authentically claim as my own.

But I am also proud. I come from a lineage who were resilient and able to adapt and create a new culture that is a hybrid of different ethnic groups. I am proud of my ancestors for not only maintaining their heritage, but for being flexible to infuse their culture with African, Amerindian, Chinese, European, Portuguese, and Spanish influences. In a country with a heterogeneous population, everyone takes part in cultural festivities and holidays even if they are from a different race or religion. I am proud because they didn't let a ruthless system destroy their spirit. My ancestors chose to find meaning and peace in their new homeland.

Nodding to Henna, I checked off 'other' and wrote the words Indo-Caribbean on the line next to it.

"Nick," I said.

"Yeah?"

"I am Guyanese."

Sticky Wicket
Krystal M. Ramroop

With one hand tightly gripping a bottle of wine, the other tugging at my fitted blue dress, I saunter past the open white iron gate and down the narrow dirt pathway—each step coordinating with the rhythmic chatter that mingles among an upbeat remix of a filmi Indian tune in the tropical air—towards the illuminated turquoise-colored bottom house.

When Cousin Rakesh heard a few months back that I'd be in Guyana for the first time to see him and his franchise team compete in the T20 Caribbean cricket tournament, he didn't hesitate to extend an invitation to me for his annual bottom house soirée at his childhood home in East Coast Demerara. I'd be foolish to miss authentic Guyanese cuisine cooked fireside, an action-packed (and emotionally charged) game of dominoes, and live chutney performances (from the local cricketers with hidden talent) that'd get the international cricketers on their feet and "wukking their waist." Earlier that day, Brenda, Rakesh's wife, insisted I accompany her to watch the team practice at the national stadium. She couldn't resist pointing out the eligible bachelors for my amusement.

The filmi tune eases into a reggae one while I dissect the array of accents from the batsmen and bowlers flooding the spacious area. My stomach begins to churn as I notice Shiva Goswami (England's finest all-rounder) standing alongside Asif Malik (Pakistan's wicket-keeper-batsman), my cousin, and another man who appears to be around my age. Their gel-slicked hair, similar attire, and synchronized laughter makes them resemble a boy band. With the exception of Asif, they each stood with one hand occupying a bottle of local beer, the other shoved casually in the front pocket of their skinny jeans. I admire how Shiva's blue button-down shirt hugs his muscles. He senses my eyes are hooked on him and permits his own to meet mine. Rakesh, Asif, and the other man follow suit. I stop dead in my tracks, conveniently in front of the staircase leading to the kitchen of the house's upper story. Before they can say anything or even make their way towards me, Brenda descends the stairs in haste.

"Is about time yuh reach!" she exclaims, interlocking her arm in mine as I hand her the bottle of wine. Quickly thanking me, she looks at her husband and company and adds over the music, "I stealing she for a minute but I go bring she back."

"You're acting like we didn't hang out at Providence earlier," I tell her as she pulls me up the staircase, Shiva and his irresistible smile slowly disappearing from my view.

Once we get into the kitchen, I'm drawn to the warm smells of fresh roti, cinnamon-spiced chicken curry, and coconut milk infused cook-up rice with an assortment of alcoholic beverages wafting in through the window shutters. A mischievous grin graces Brenda's face, regaining my attention.

"Wah mek?"

"Rakesh teammate asking for you steady steady," she says in a low whisper, propping herself against the counter. "The one who was smiling up at you juss now."

"Shiva?" I ask, folding my arms across my chest as I brace my body against one of the dining table chairs. "Because he could ask for me all—"

"No, no, not he. I mean, he was asking for you too but the other one. Brian," she tells me.

"Uh-huh, so?"

"'Memba when yuh sey yuh na wan be nobody ticket to 'Merica?" I nod. "Well, Brian barn an' grow dey so every ting done set."

I laugh. "You're trying to hook me up with him?"

"Yes! Yuh prappa slow, gyal!" I roll my eyes, giving her a half-smile. "I done put in ah good word," she adds.

I straighten my posture, refraining from pouncing on her. "You did what?"

"I tell he you is smart and funny and yuh roti roun' and yuh like—"

"Oh gosh, Brenda," I say. "My roti is not round, I'm not interested in Brian, and...I need a beer."

Motioning to her to leave the kitchen with me, Shiva and I nearly run into each other on the staircase, Rakesh trailing behind him.

"Hi," Shiva says, standing on the step below us with a grip on my waist to steady me.

My hands instinctively latch onto his broad shoulders. "Shiva Goswami," I whisper, our faces nearly touching. I absorb his kempt black hair and beard, golden brown orbs, and soft tamarind colored skin.

"Yes, and your cousin," Rakesh announces, as Brenda pries my hands off of Shiva's shoulders.

Shiva loosens his grip on me and steps aside so Rakesh can stand beside him to embrace me.

"Hi Captain," I sing, hugging him. "Thanks again for the invite."

"Of course, anything for my baby cousin," he says with a Creole twang, pulling back to pinch my cheeks. "Shiv and I just came to get the instruments. I sort of let it slip to Shane and Haniff that you sing chutney songs and now they're itching to show you their dance moves."

"The South African bowlers, right?" I ask. He nods. "Oh gosh, Rakesh. Singing and carrying a tune are two different things you know."

"Denial nah suit you," Brenda says, giving me a quick nudge before beckoning Rakesh in an exaggerated American accent. "You come and get the harmonium. I'll help you bring out the dhantal."

Not giving Rakesh a chance to answer, she slips her hand in his and hurriedly pulls him into the house, leaving Shiva and I standing alone on the staircase to bask in a chutney track laced with sexual innuendos. Our gazes lock on each other and I feel my heart racing with the tempo of the dholak.

"I've been on this team for four years now. How come we've never met before?" he asks, his British accent smooth as condensed milk.

I shrug, motioning to our clothing. "How come no one got the memo to wear blue tonight?" He fails at suppressing his chuckle and I can't help but join him. "I've seen you play on television," I admit. "That must count for something, right?"

"Sure, but since you can 'carry a tune,' I think what would really count is if you dedicate a song to me."

I smile and in the best British accent I can muster, I tell him, "I'll see what I can do." His eyes glint in both satisfaction and amazement. "Anyways, I reckon you should be off helping Rakesh and Brenda," I add.

"Oh, c'mon, you can't unexpectedly match my accent with such elegance and expect me to give up easily on you."

"You wish you could handle this Caribbean spice, Goswami," I say, slipping away from him.

Reaching the bottom stair, I turn back to look at him before completely disappearing from his view.

"I probably did handle all of your spice in another life," he calls after me. "I'm Hindu after all."

I laugh to myself, the moment all too surreal. I continue along the narrow pathway. As I maneuver my way through the cricketers, muttering a polite 'hello' to each I encounter, my eyes land on the two large coolers at the end of the food table. I find Asif, Shane Taylor, and Haniff Ul-Haq dishing out cook-up. Brian and Mark Narine, a Trinidadian all-rounder, are seated on cheap white plastic chairs near the ongoing domino game, deep in concentration. Brian quickly offers a warm smile in my direction, to which I return. I sink my hand in the cooler containing alcoholic beverages, shifting the ice cubes for a Banks Shandy. I pull the bottle out and grab the cap opener, contemplating where to sit in the sea of testosterone. Brian appears at my side. I watch how the soft white light from the bottom house ceiling reflects on his glistening brown skin. He runs his slender fingers through his tousled black hair with one hand, the other reaching into the same cooler. He clasps both hands around the wet Banks Beer bottle, places it near his mouth, giving it a little twist, and swiftly uncaps it with his teeth.

"Too good for the opener?" I ask before I take a sip of my beer.

He shakes his head. "The things I do to make an impression. I might have to see a dentist later."

I laugh. "Consider me impressed. And sorry if you've ruined your teeth."

He smiles and takes a seat on the empty bench near the shed, beckoning me to join him. I tug at my dress and obey him, placing my beer on the ground near my feet. I fold my hands on my lap, hoping to prevent myself from running them across his strong jawline.

He shifts his body, turning to me. "So, you're into cricket?" he asks casually.

I nod happily. "I'm still learning the laws of the game. I grew up watching it but never understood the basics."

"Let me guess, you were told it was like baseball without actually understanding baseball?"

I laugh. "How'd you know? Same boat, eh?"

He chuckles, nodding. "My dad and mamoo would rave about their "old-time" days during the village matches they played in. I couldn't seem to avoid the game. It runs in our blood."

"So cricket was bound to be a budding addiction," I say.

He smirks, studying me before uttering, "You writers have such a way with words."

"How'd you know I'm a writer?" I ask before adding, "Wait, don't answer that."

He grins. "I hope you don't mind me asking about you." I shake my head. "It can be a little intimidating out here as the only American on the team who's still trying to understand the homeland culture."

"Story of my life, minus the team," I mutter. "It's your first time in Guyana?"

He nods. "Auntie Brenda told me it was your first time too and I was like, 'oh me mama,' someone I can finally bond with.'"

I giggle. "How come I ain't see you at practice earlier?"

"My flight got delayed so I got to the hotel later than expected," he explains.

"Good ol' West Indian Standard Time," I say, before my delayed response kicked in. "Hold up, did you say Auntie Brenda?"

"Yeah, she's my auntie, Rakesh is my uncle." My eyes widen, and immediately I pop up from my seat. "Wait, what? Why does it feel like we're not bonding anymore?" he asks.

His arm brushes against my leg as he stands up. I quickly grab my beer bottle and revert to the end of the food table, nearly bumping into Shiva.

"Hey there," he says, gripping my arms. "Did you decide what song you're dedicating to me?"

"Shiva, sorry...I—"

"Goswami, like you got a thing for my cousin or what?" Rakesh asks over the music, sauntering towards us as laughter resounds from his teammates. "I've already set up the instruments so—"

"It's chutney bacchanal time!" Shane yells, gaining a few cheers.

"Is what you know about bacchanal, eh?" Mark asks with the dhantal in his grip.

Brian looks at me in horror before we break eye contact and turn to look at Brenda.

The Girl Drinks

Jihan Ramroop

He stares at me like he knows me. In some ways he does; not a whole lot, but he's seen me more than my own parents. My own friends.

A strange feeling grows between my heart. Not love, but his brother? Something I do not know the name of.

And it is at this moment I confuse the two things. Love and desire. I want to be loved. But this is not it. This is desire.

"I'll drop you," he says.

"Okay."

He grabs his keys and heads to the door.

I follow him and wait for him to lock up. He turns to me and smiles, kinda. His scruffy beard makes me mad. Makes me remember how old he is, how he shouldn't be doing this. Flirting with me, liking me. But he does, and I let him.

The thing continues to grow in my stomach and I know now this is not desire; this is something else. Regret? It tastes like nothing.

I do not have time to rescind my offer. We are in the car in a couple steps. We drive in silence, the radio is off. Just the air conditioning and my too loud heart. He stops just a few houses before my own.

"Thank you," I say.

He looks at me. "You're welcome." As he speaks, I feel a hand on my knee. Just like that, one second not there, then there.

I freeze.

My heart beat blocks out any other noise. It drowns it. Drowns me. I cannot speak. I want to move, speak, and breathe. But I cannot.

"You're leaving tomorrow," he says.

I nod. Trying to find some words, but nothing comes out.

The street is lined with sleeping houses, all the lights off. I can see my own house from here, but I know it's no use. The danger has already come.

"Have fun at college," he says.

He's looking at me but I won't look back. Finally he relents.

The carlock clicks open and I realize I've known it was locked the whole ride. I pull the handle, exit the vehicle. I move towards my house. I am no longer here, but back in that night. Tears rush down my face and I slap them away. My parents are watching TV through the blinds. I hear his tires screech, my parents look towards the window at me. I smile.

Everything's gonna be okay.

***

He smiles. "Come take one drink."

"I ... shouldn't."

Instead, though, my body sits, like it has a mind of its own. He pours two glasses, no chaser. I wince as it burns down my throat.

"Yuh guh drink plenty in college. My son did."

"I don't really drink," I say.

"Don't worry, I won't tell your father...or mother."

He gets up, puts on a song from his stereo. It's a mix between chutney and Hindi. A chune.

"Oh meh almost forgot!" He pulls out an envelope. "Yuh last paycheck." He smiles as he hands it to me.

"Thank you." I hesitated.

He sits beside me and it's so effortless how his hand finds my knee. Like two long lost friends.

"Open it," he tells me.

"Now?" I watch Ramcharran, the other coworker, through the glass windows in the next office. He waves and I realize what this must look like. I move.

Ramcharran doesn't stop, doesn't show his face for more than the two seconds it takes him to cross to the door. Yet it plays in my head through the night.

The song plays louder in the background. I look at him and he smiles again, but suddenly I want to move. Run, breathe. But I don't. Instead I open the envelope. It's cash, like he always pays me. But it's too much. I tell him this. He shakes his head, pouring another glass.

"You're going to college. You need it." He raises his glass and waits for me to do the same.

It clinks and my heartbeat falls away between the music and the liquor. I am not here anymore. I fall against the couch. I smile back.

My body betrays me. It doesn't move when he comes closer. It doesn't run. It doesn't react the way I want it to. Instead, I am still. He smiles and it's all I remember from that night and for many more nights as I down shots of rum, tequila, vodka and whiskey.

I try to erase it, try to recreate it. Maybe if I drink more it will taste better—make the memory fade, make me feel good.

It was not your fault. It was not your fault. It was not your fault.

But I was there with him. I drank with him.

I stayed with him.

The voice tries to save me. But I don't want to be saved. I want to drink.

***

3 months later

I was already drunk when I saw him. I already had half a bottle of tequila that I saved from college. I drank it in the car ride here in the back of my parents' SUV, disguised as a bottle of grape juice. I don't speak so they can't suspect anything and I chew on Tridents so they can't smell me. I didn't even bother to protest when I heard whose Christmas party it was. No. Instead I slowly got drunk as my parents got ready, finally pulling on an old dress and sweater. I put on a little mascara and some foundation. *Look normal. Feel normal.* This bottle will last me till about 12 o'clock. But a little more couldn't hurt.

It is then in the kitchen that I see him. Good thing I already have the rum poured in my cup of soda. But instantly, like it did that night, my body betrays me. Heat and water enter my eyes, teasing tears to release any minute.

Fuck, fuck, fuck.

I bite my tongue so it hurts harder. Down the alcohol so it goes down faster. It stings for a second and then I feel it in my stomach, feel the bile rise in my throat. He stares at me through the crowd, his eyes and lips flat and straight. His wife joins him. He breaks his gaze and I am free.

I move through the crowd and spot my parents laughing with a couple in the living room. There's some younger kids, too young to stay at home but old enough to supervise themselves playing in the basement. I'm heading there when I feel someone looking at me.

The boy stares at me like he knows me and I him. His eyes beckon me like a stranger, like a friend. I want to look away, find some other focus, but I can't. Everyone else falls away. Without thought, I smile at him. Flash my teeth. He grins back. He meets me at the kitchen counter.

"How are you doing that?" he asks.

"What?"

"So, secretly and successfully stealing the rum?"

"It's easy, no one suspects the girl...but the girl drinks," I say.

"The girl drinks..." he feigns shock, raising both hands to his face.

I laugh. "Yeah, she drinks and is such a mess. But it's a secret. Shh..."

"A secret?" He smiles. I feel my heart get tight. "I won't tell," he whispers.

"Ok," I whisper back. "Good."

"Let's get away," he whispers still. I smile in response.

We exit through the back door. I feel eyes on me, but I don't look. I don't care at this point; the alcohol is in my bones. The cool night smacks us with a welcome and I hear the chutney stifle as he pulls in the door. My ears adjust to the crickets gaffing in the night.

"Your parents inside?" he asks as we walk towards the road.

"Yep... yours?" I try walking in a straight line on the driveway's curb.

"Yeah, you've probably seen them—"

"Oh god, I hope we're not family," I laugh.

He laughs and it sounds like a song. "Why? You like me?"

"Yuh wish!" I smile at him but then look away at the night. It's so calm. Almost sobering.

I sit on the curb where the road kisses the grass. I feel him settle next to me. We don't say anything. I feel him look at me, then stare straight at the dark houses in front of us. A silent dead suburb.

Where was I this time last night?

Getting drunk with Sammy and Meena.

Oh god I miss them. Love them. Want them here with me now. I need to be drunker than this.

"What are you thinking about?" he asks.

I turn to look at him. "Time travel and the possibilities if I could just finish inventing my damn time machine."

He smiles and I fall a little in love.

"You don't like the party?" I ask.

He shakes his head. "They're all the same. Get drunk. Go home. Do it all again."

"True." I nod.

"Are you drunk enough?" he asks.

"Huh?"

"Oh, don't play sober. I've seen you drink since you got here."

"You've seen me?" I'm surprised.

"You've been emptying the liquor bottles every time you stepped into the kitchen. We should hide the liquor," he says.

"So, I'm a little drunk...but I could be more." I shrug.

He holds his cup out.

I shake my head. "Juta." He laughs.

***

She smiles but takes the cup anyway. She looks into it, like she's studying the world and then nothing at all.

"Okay, I really hope we're not family," she says.

She stares at me, her big brown eyes so full of light. Like the moon is reflecting in them.

"Why yuh wanna get married?" I joke.

Her eyes go big. "You read my mind."

I laugh and the sound pierces the quiet night.

"Man, I wish I was more drunk for this," she says.

"Drunk for what?" I ask.

She leans over and then kisses me. Her lips barely press against mine, like she's unsure. We break and look at each other. Then we kiss again. The world pauses. The crickets stop. Everything falls away. She pulls back to look at me.

"So, yeah, I hope we're not family."

"I hope so too," I say.

A door opens and old chutney music stumbles into our quiet night. Someone probably wanting some air or leaving. I'm aware of how close I am to her. Our bodies are mere millimeters apart. She looks to see who it is and her face falls. Likes she's sober and sad all at once. All alcohol drained from her system in a second. I turn my head back to look too. I see him.

"What yuh doing out here when everybody inside?" he asks.

He walks closer and I feel her shift.

"Oh... hi." He stops a few yards from us. His drink is in his hand. His eyes fall on her.

***

I want to run. I want to hide. I want to yell. But I cannot do any of those things. Instead, I am paralyzed, or worse, I have control of my body, I just can't move it. I look at the man in front of me. The boy next to me. My mind tells me something but my body is slow to comprehend.

"This is my dad, Dad this is..."

"We met," I choke out.

I look between them. Father and son. Father and son. Father and son. I try to smile. Talk. Do anything. We stare at each other and it seems like the night stares with us. The breeze, the crickets and the mosquito on my ankle holding its mouth from biting me.

All the alcohol in my stomach is ready to come out like nice vomit into a toilet's mouth. But it's in my throat and I can't stop it.

I throw up.

This is Not a Self Portrait

Ashley Anthony

"You know, Leela, it feels rather repetitive of you to make different versions of self-portraits for your assignments every week," says Desiree. She tosses her long, newly-dyed purple hair over her shoulder, popping her gum, as if for emphasis, as she shrugs at Leela.

"Yeah, it's, like, fine to do once in a while, but maybe, like, try something more daring!" Jamie chimes in.

He swirls the ice around in his cup of iced coffee before taking a sip.

"You know? Like how Alexa did this week, using blues to illustrate the emotional state of the woman in her painting!"

Leela shrinks at the negative attention her classmates give her. Her brows furrow as she counts on her fingers. *How many more weeks are left in this course,* she wonders, while nodding blankly at her peers' critique.

Leela thinks she hears one of her classmates say something about the subject's straight, flowing hair as a representation of Leela and her growth as a person. She regards her piece for a moment, reaching up to tuck a stray curl behind her ear. She takes a deep breath, mustering enough patience to speak to her classmates.

"Um..." she hesitates. "Why do you think it's a self-portrait?"

A heavy silence fills the room. Her classmates look at one another, waiting to see who will speak first.

"Well," Jamie scratches the shaved side of his head. "It's just that all of your paintings look the same..." he trails off, looking pleadingly at their professor for help.

Professor Edwards clears her throat. "Leela, I think what your classmates are trying to say—" She waves a heavily adorned hand in the air. "It seems you're making safe, comfortable choices. I would love to see something wildly out of your comfort zone." She turns her attention to the rest of the class, changing the subject to diffuse the tension. "For our next class, I would like each of you to choose a color palette you have not used before in a previous assignment. Same topic as assigned."

She splays her fingers in a small arc away from her shoulders, miming a small explosion, jingling the bracelets on her wrists. "Consumption. A juxtaposition of the body and food," Professor Edwards beams. "Have a good day, everyone!"

With that announcement, class ends. Each student returns to their workspace and packs their things before leaving the room. Leela hesitates, casting quick glances between Professor Edwards' cluttered desk and the exit. She lingers behind in the classroom while her classmates leave. She packs her belongings slowly, placing each pencil into her case and turning page after page of her sketchbook until she gets near enough to the front cover to shut it completely. She fidgets with her things, stacking them in different arrangements, but never actually placing them in her bag.

"Is everything all right, Leela?" Professor Edwards asks, glancing up from her desk.

She takes off her reading glasses and makes her way over to Leela's workspace, her cardigan and skirt floating around her.

"Yeah." Leela absent-mindedly flips the pages of her sketchbook. A graphite-smeared sheet of paper towel slips out, fluttering to the floor. "Actually no, Professor. I'm honestly confused by today's crit."

Professor Edwards leans against the nearest worktable and folds her arms. She tilts her head to the side and nods at Leela to continue. Leela picks up the paper towel, crumpling it in her hands.

"It's just, everyone seems to think I only paint self-portraits. I haven't done a self-portrait since our intro assignment." Leela tucks a curl behind her ear and continues slowly, looking away from her professor. "Every single crit day, I get at least three comments from the others saying that my subjects are me," she taps her fingers on the table. "Even the ones where we all used the same model for our pieces!"

"Leela, your work is good in the technical sense. You are a skilled artist," Professor Edwards says, leaning heavily against the table's edge, twisting a gaudy ring around her index finger.

"But?" Leela asks.

Professor Edwards sighs, smoothing her spindly, mottled hands over her gray-streaked hair.

"But, this course isn't only about developing and honing technical skills!" She stands up straight, throwing her arms out to the side. "I want to see you taking more risks with your subject matter. Surely, you have much more to say than," she makes air quotes, "'I'm an Indian woman who isn't entirely at home in my own body.'"

Leela's face burns. She swallows hard. "That's not..." she starts. "I'm Guyanese...."

"There is a place for striking and recognizable style, but so far, the only aspect of your pieces that stands out is the women you paint," she picks at a loose thread on her cardigan sleeve, "who just so happen to look much like you. You need to develop your artistic voice."

Leela clenches her jaw and drops the crumpled paper towel. She yanks the zipper of her backpack open and shoves her things inside. She lowers her head slightly, a few stray curls falling in front of her face.

"I just..."

Her professor quirks an eyebrow. "Yes?"

She closes her bag and looks squarely into the professor's eyes. "I don't see how my painting of brown people is any different from other students painting every variation of white women under the sun. Or using light-haired, light-eyed figures and literally painting them to represent innocence and goodness and positivity."

"You see—" Professor Edwards begins.

"Any message I put into my work gets glossed over..." Leelas's voice begins to crack. "No one can get past the fact that the figures in them," she takes a shaky breath, her voice raising, "happen to look different than what they're used to seeing."

"Leela—"

"Like," she snaps. "What's with the praise of *blues* in Alexa's painting to 'illustrate the emotional state of their subject?'" Leela jerks her bag from its resting place on her seat. "What *isn't* safe and comfortable about those choices? Blue for sadness? Oh, *that's* never been done before." She scoffs. "Does that say anything about Alexa's voice?"

"Leela. This isn't about Alexa's painting; it's about all of yours," Professor Edwards says sharply. "If you cannot stomach the critiques offered to you by your peers, how do you imagine you will fare in the art world? My opinion?" She clicks her tongue, "You won't."

Leela steps backwards, dropping her bag to the ground in shock.

"Have a good rest of the week, Leela. I look forward to seeing something *different* from you next week." Professor Edwards turns, heels clicking against the floor, and leaves the room without another word.

Leela shakes her head and snatches her bag from the floor. She blinks away tears and squeezes her eyes shut before taking a deep breath. On her way out of the classroom, she stops in front of the light switch. She hesitates before finally switching the light off.

***

At home, Leela sits cross-legged on the floor of her bedroom beside her hard, plastic desk chair. A plush rug cushions her from the hardwood floor. Half-used sheets of paper, scribbled with ideas for her next assignment, litter the floor around her. The cream-colored walls are taped and tacked with unframed prints. One wall is a collage of sticky notes, used as a large to-do list, growing smaller and smaller by the day as the semester draws to a close. In less than a month, the semester would be over.

"Consumption? What a stupid, pretentious topic," she giggles. "This assignment is consuming *me*." She grabs the nearest discarded sheet and inspects it before crumpling it up and throwing it against her to-do list wall.

"I can't believe these people." She slaps her palm against the hard floor. "They're so distracted by a different complexion that they can't even view my ideas properly."

She sits up straighter. "Professor Edwards has some nerve, too! What does she even mean by 'not at home in my own body?'" She grabs her sketchbook, flips to an unmarked page, and begins to sketch furiously, tearing the page with the roughness of her pencil-strokes. She turns the page and starts over. "I'll show them something that stands out."

***

The next class begins with group critiques rather than ending with them. According to Professor Edwards, changing when critique takes place during class time is an exercise in perspective. Critiques at the beginning of class allow students to take advice immediately to heart, whereas critiques at the end offer the opportunity to sit with the new information and decide whether to use the advice or not.

Leela's classmates gather around the bulletin board. Every single one was populated by thin, white, conventionally attractive women being consumed by or composed of various desserts. One featured a woman clinging to a neon red cherry submerged in a vanilla milkshake. Leela folds her arms and takes in the scene. She notices the title card beneath that painting: *Untitled - Desiree Lewis*. She rolls her eyes at the display.

"Of course," she muttered under her breath. What could they possibly criticize about her work now that it fits in with everyone else's?

Professor Edwards starts with the first piece on the left and moves along down the line. Leela's peers lavish each other with compliments. Looking at the other students' pieces, Leela begins to lose confidence in her plan. Her piece is barely distinguishable from the rest. Why is Jamie's painting of a woman pulling a slice of red velvet cake out of her chest so special? What's so clever about her painting of a near-nude woman covered in pastries? Leela's stomach turns thinking about how boring and cliché her painting turned out. This isn't *her*. Her heart races and her palms sweat the closer the class comes to her piece. Her breath catches in her throat when Professor Edwards calls the class's attention to her work.

A stunned silence fills the classroom. Jamie breaks the tension first.

"Um, no offense, but I had no idea you made that, Leela." The rest of her classmates murmur in agreement.

Leela squints, glaring at her classmate. "I, uh...It just doesn't seem like you. It feels really bland compared to what you've been doing," Jamie stumbles.

He looks awkwardly between Leela and her painting. "It's nice to see you, like, switch it up, though! Your blonde lady really, like, pops against, um, the dark baking tray."

Leela chews on her bottom lip, keeping herself from speaking, and nods.

Another student, Lucy, pipes up. "This feels like you gave into the idea of being an artist instead of actually being an artist. This looks like an image that an artist in a stock photo would have made." She chews the tip of her pencil. "I mean, what's with the cookies and donuts covering her up?"

With that last comment from Lucy, the entire class erupts in overlapping chatter. Leela clenches her fists tightly, digging her nails into the skin of her palms. The words "unoriginal," "boring," and "lack of creative spirit" echo throughout the classroom. Professor Edwards looks at her, shaking her head in disappointment. As she looks away, even her dangling earrings seem disappointed in Leela.

Leela grabs her backpack roughly and slings it over her shoulder. She stalks up to the bulletin board, yanking her painting down, before turning to face the class.

"Every single one of these is just as boring," she waves her piece wildly. "You think a naked woman with literal melons for boobs is clever?" She sucks her teeth sharply. "You're all full of it!"

Leela huffs, irritated by her classmates' blank faces, and storms out of the room.

***

Two weeks had passed since Leela stormed out of class. Her professor had reached out twice: the first, to reprimand her for the "unprofessional outburst." The second, a reminder that final projects and critiques would be due the following week. Her final project was due in two days and she had not yet started.

Leela's usually tidy room had devolved into a mess of sketchbooks and paintings. She grimaces looking around her room, her eyes light on her consumption assignment. She glares at the painting and feels heat rising to her cheeks. She stomps out of her room towards the kitchen and pulls a knife from the dish rack, before returning to her room and slamming the door behind her. She grips the knife tightly, her chest rising and falling quickly. She lunges towards her papers, dropping the knife beside her, and begins to rip and tear and shred them in her hands. She pulls her canvases close to her and picks up the knife, hesitating for just a moment, before plunging the blade down, shredding and mangling them. She tosses the knife away, sighing as she throws the scraps in the air, like confetti made of failure and humiliation. A guttural sob escapes her as she roughly brushes the scraps from her hair and clothing. She flops onto her bed and buries her face into her pillow sobbing.

She had made a mistake. Her parents were right. She should have gone to pharmacy school, done what her parents wanted, instead of risking her heart and their support. She was already over halfway through her degree. The last few years of her life were a waste.

Leela rolls over onto her back. There is no turning back now. Whether she fails this class or not, she is going to finish what she started. This is what she wanted, and she was going to give it everything she had. She sits up and wipes the tears from her face. She gathers the scraps scattered around her room and begins to work. She has one last idea.

***

One by one, the students enter the classroom and set up their final projects along the display board. Once each work is set up, a reverent hush falls over the room. Professor Edwards steps to the front, layered necklaces clinking together. She faces the students and clears her throat.

"I'm so pleased to see what you've done with your final projects. The creative spirit is overwhelming in this room," she beams.

"Just as we've done before, I want to hear the opinions of your peers before the artist has a chance to explain their concept. This final project was deliberately left open-ended so each of you could take what you've learned these past months and make something that *truly* demonstrates your artistic voice."

Professor Edwards moves to the side of the room and gestures for the class to begin. Leela feels a different attitude coming from her peers during this discussion and critique. For the first time, their comments are constructive.

Rather than focusing only on aesthetics, her classmates discussed thematic choices and execution. As the class worked their way towards her final project, Leela tenses up in her seat, anxiety getting the better of her. She quietly chimes in with her own feedback for the other students before her painting lands in the spotlight.

Desiree speaks up first. "I'm incredibly impressed with the concept of this piece. I can feel Leela's frustration with the prevailing state of the art world and how it's both literally and figuratively tearing her work apart."

Desiree looks over at Leela and smiles. "Amazing job!" she says, clapping her hands together.

"Yeah, this is unlike anything you've brought to class before," Alexa nods in approval. "I like the collage aspect of this painting. Mixed media is *so* in right now. Destroying your own work to create something? So cool. Really thought-provoking."

Jamie adds, "Yeah! Your subject doesn't look like you at all!" Leela grimaces. "Like, I mean, it looks like there's elements of you and your feelings, but it's not *just* a self-portrait like all your other ones." Leela tucks a loose curl behind her ear and clasps her hands together in her lap, keeping quiet.

Her classmates never praised her work before. But, even now, they could only manage to deliver backhanded compliments. Leela closes her eyes and pinches the bridge of her nose.

Professor Edwards takes an extra moment to regard Leela's painting before turning her attention to Leela.

"You have outdone yourself with this, Leela. This is exactly what I meant when I spoke with you about taking more risks." She pauses for a moment. "Your choice to craft a disembodied figure from your own dismembered work is nothing short of brilliant."

Professor Edwards claps her hands together three times before extending her hands out to the class. "Leela, I think it's rather clear what your intentions are with this painting. Well thought out and executed. But I'm curious," she gestures towards Leela's painting, "you left the title section blank. Surely you can't leave this piece as 'Untitled!' Have you come up with a name for it?"

Leela leans forward in her chair, barely suppressing a smirk.

"I think I'll call it 'Self Portrait.'"

To Hell with Tradition

Tiffany Manbodh

Some say there's nothing like a mother's love, but this story is far from it. Myra's mother made her regret the day she was ever born. At the age of sixteen, most girls were going to the movies with their friends and exploring different shades of lipstick. However, her life was far from these experiences.

Myra was almost done sweeping the floor of her family's living room when her mother entered unexpectedly. Her mother had just received a marriage proposal from her best friend, asking for Myra's hand in marriage to Sushant. Her mother's face was filled with gladness, her cheeks reaching her lower lash line as if they hadn't met in what seemed like forever. She informed Myra that she was so delighted by the offer that she had taken it upon herself to accept the proposal on her daughter's behalf.

Myra thought this was just another one of her mother's delusional tricks. She completely dismissed it and went about her business sweeping the floor. A few days later, while Myra was getting dressed, her mother came in and repeated the same words.

"You will be getting married to my best friend's son and I cannot wait!" Myra felt her limbs become cold all of a sudden.

Her silence encapsulated the entire room while she stared back at her mother's gleaming eyes. She wondered to herself why her mother was still continuing this charade. After all, Myra felt that it was an awful thing to be joking about. Her plans for her life at sixteen did not include being married off and made into a housewife. She had always dreamed of having her own small business and merchandising the sweet treats she created in the family's small kitchen.

Sunday arrived. The day of rest and relaxation. A big pot of Guyanese cook-up rice now simmered on the stove while Indian tunes filled the space. Sunday was always Myra's happy day because it was the only time she got to relax in the hammock within one of the bedrooms. She rocked herself into tranquility, but was transported out of it when she heard unfamiliar footsteps entering the home. Her mother's voice greeted the best friend whose son she was supposedly going to be wed to. At this moment, a tiny part of Myra still hoped that this was all a joke, that her mother's best friend was just visiting to drop off some homemade sweets, which she loved showing off at the tea time meetings held once a month in their village. This was a time where a handful of the women in the community gathered and would rave about their children's accomplishments or sulk for their lack of progress.

Her mother began to laugh, saying what a joyous occasion it was going to be that she and her best friend were going to become family. It was then that Myra realized that this was no façade, that her mother was determined to marry her off to some stranger she had never met. Myra stood up from the hammock and her mind began to race. Anxiety of what was to come came like an uninvited guest, and before she knew it, she found it harder to breathe.

She felt like she was going to faint. This all felt like a dream which was not seeming to pass. Myra laid flat on the cold floor, her spine trying to find solace against the rocky surface. She slowly tried to reassemble her thoughts, one by one.

"I am okay," she whispered the words of affirmation to herself, hoping to signal her body to revert back to calmness, everything which she wasn't currently feeling.

Her mom must have sensed something because she came dancing into the room to announce that Myra would be getting married the following month.

A few days later, the mother of the soon-to-be groom returned to fix a wedding date that her pandit thought was auspicious after comparing the astrological signs of the soon-to-be-wedded couple. Everything was set. The finality of it all crippled the dreams that Myra had held close to her heart for so long. She felt powerless in this new predicament. There was no way she was going to tell her mother what was really on her mind. She didn't have much of a choice, or so she felt. She knew the nature of her mother; she spoke in tones of commandment. She was the kind of woman that always had to have the last word so there was no way that Myra was going to question her judgement. She looked to her mother as a strong father figure since she played both roles, being a single mother to six children.

Myra did not want to disappoint her mother so she went along with everything that was going to take place in the coming weeks. To her surprise, Sushant stopped by after his work at the post office one day unannounced.

Myra was startled when she saw him walking down the path their house was situated on. That day, he stayed a long while. There was small talk. Most of the time, he gazed at his soon-to-be bride, his eyes glistening with desire. Myra was very quiet and shy, not saying much unless he asked a question. Eventually, what seemed like an eternity had passed and Sushant went along on his way. He returned a few days after for a short while to acquaint himself with the girl who he would eventually be coexisting with.

The invitations were sent out to family, close friends, neighbors and so on. A few days before the wedding, Myra was at the kitchen sink washing dishes when she heard a stranger's voice calling out to her from the front door. She rushed to see who it could be as she wasn't expecting anyone. A lady, her skin an olive hue, in a green ruffled dress, stood outside. Her body language revealed an eagerness to tell Myra something urgent. She informed Myra the man she was about to marry was her ex son-in-law. Myra didn't know how to respond. What could she possibly say to this lady? At one point, she was thankful for any excuse to tell her mother to call this whole wedding off. On the other hand, she knew the wrath that her mother would have waiting for her if she didn't marry Sushant.

A few days later, Sushant came over to visit Myra's house again as usual. This time, she was fuming inside as to why he didn't tell her he was married before. She brought over the tea and sat down for their afternoon tea time. She began to crack her knuckles, relieving any anxiety present. As he picked up his cup to drink, she asked him how come he never mentioned a previous marriage. Sushant's entire facial expression changed. He was shocked. He thought to himself how she could have known. He tried to maintain his composure as best as he could. After a few deep breaths, he confirmed that he had been married but things didn't work out. He and his wife separated as a result. Little did he know, the mother had also told Myra that her daughter was pregnant with his child. Here Myra was about to marry a man that her mother had arranged for her, not knowing he had a child on the way. She was angry that she was now learning these things less than a week before they were to be wedded.

The wedding day arrived. They had a traditional Indian wedding ceremony, with close relatives and neighbors invited. Myra had not prepared herself for what was soon to be revealed in her new husband's habits. A few months passed by. Marriage life had been sweet, filled with constant love making and learning about each other. However, things began to take a different turn. Sushant started going out late at night, leaving his wife at home alone. She soon learned about his drinking and smoking habits, something very new to her. She didn't know how to cope with all of this new information. Another month went by and she was pregnant. Myra had no idea what to do. She felt helpless at times. When the time came to deliver the baby, she was unable to go to a hospital and delivered her baby at home, with a midwife nurse present.

Not long after, she found out that his previous wife had also given birth and planned to take Sushant to court to pay child support. Myra endured many sleepless nights, tossing and turning as she thought about the way her life had turned out. She didn't visit her mom after the baby was born. She was too ashamed of what her life had become with this husband of hers. They kept in contact through the telephone, and whenever her mom asked how she was doing, she would always say she was doing just fine.

One night, Sushant came home from a late night of partying with his friends and Myra sat him down, telling him her feelings about his drinking. She explained she didn't like the way he behaved when he imbibed. His expression became livid as he proceeded to undo his belt. He began to beat her.

Myra did not socialize as much, afraid that people would notice her bruises and ask questions. She focused on taking care of their child and tried not to think about the abuse. However, the abuse continued multiple times after he came home late and drunk.

Years passed by and they had more children. Myra was unhappy with whatever bits were left of their marriage. When the neighbors informed her that her husband was having an affair, it didn't surprise her. He would be gone the entire weekend at times, leaving her with the children. He said it was work related, but Myra knew it was more than that. But, she didn't leave him because she was afraid of what her mother would say. She began dreaming of a man that had characteristics opposite those of her husband.

One morning, Myra went to the market to pick up some herbs for the cook-up dish she was going to make. The shawl that she wore over her shoulder fell by accident, revealing the bruises. The gentleman selling her the vegetables noticed and pulled her to the side to have a conversation. He asked her how she got those bruises and she completely broke down in tears in front of him. He just held her and tried to comfort her as best as he could. Myra apologized for crying, but the wise man said it was no big deal. He told her that she could talk to him about anything at any time. Myra visited the market every day after that to speak with him, enjoying being around someone other than the ladies who gossip in the village. After some time together, Myra had developed a fondness for the market stall guy, Kabir. They began spending time together near the sea, having tea. He could see through her pain and wanted to give her a happy life, despite his current financial circumstances.

Sushant had threatened Myra's life after another one of his many drunken nights; she decided the time had arrived to leave him. She completely disregarded what her mother would think. Spending valuable time with Kabir allowed her to see life from a different perspective. His compassionate character made her believe in the love she often watched in Bollywood films. One day, while her husband was at work, Kabir came to get her and the children. She would leave her house never to return to Sushant again.

Years passed by and Myra was happy. She had found her dream man. Kabir treated her children with fairness and loved them so much that they never wanted to return to their dad's home. In fact, they called Kabir 'Daddy' and would look forward to the goodies he brought when he came home from work. Myra didn't bother calling her mom. She knew from this moment on, she had to start living for herself, and made sure her children were loved and cared for. She said, 'to hell with tradition' as it had caused her nothing but suffering prior. Myra embodied a new mentality that sought to empower women and take them out of bad marriages like her own. She attended support groups and learned so much that she decided to start her own support group in her new village as well. Her goal was to ensure all of the ladies would be able to benefit and be educated on topics such as relationships, toxic behaviors, and mental health. She had found her calling.

When You Can't Go Home: Journey of Tracing Ancestry and Wanting to Visit my Indian Homeland as a Muslim Descendant of *Musalman* Indentured Labourers During the Backdrop of Anti-Muslim Violence under India's *Hindutva* and Hindu Supremacist BJP Government[1]

Karimah Rahman

---

[1] Some parts of this short story have been inspired and drawn from the authors article *Unpacking Indian Arrival Day as the Descendant of Muslim Indentured Labourers* published in 2020 in Caribbean Muslims: News, History, Culture and Religion (https://www.caribbeanmuslims.com/unpacking-indian-arrival-day-as-the-descendant-of-muslim-indentured-labourers). This fictional short story (some numbers/dates and locations have been fictionalized as well) is not meant to represent the lived experiences of all Muslim indentured labourers or their descendants and is inspired from the intersectional positionality of the author and their research, with the intent to capture ancestry invizibilized, marginalized and silenced in Indo-Caribbean (and Indentured Diasporic) spaces. The author fictionalized select information on her ancestors out of fear of naming real locations due to her decolonial and radically critical work on *Hindutva* and Hindu Supremacy in the Indentured/Indo-Caribbean diaspora. The ancestry traced in this short story is purposefully mentioned as being maternal and through the position of womxn ancestors since paternal tracing of ancestry is more easily accessible. Therefore maternal tracing of ancestry, womxn ancestors voices and oral stories should be amplified and no longer marginalized in Indentured Diasporic and Indo-Caribbean spaces.

National Archives of Guyana (June 2018)

I take a deep breath, the moment is finally here. My heart races as at last I was standing in the National Archives of Guyana. I peer around the room, taking in the scenery. The walls are bright green and the air is musty and old.

"Wuh we ah look fuh here so," yells *Chacha*[2].

"It's the *Immigration Ordinance: Register of Births*," I yell. "Daddy, help *Chacha* na," I say louder.

My daddy walks over to *Chacha* and the archivist.

"What year was *Ma*[3] born?" I ask.

"1930 on June third," says Daddy.

"Do you have the Register of Births in the county of Berbice for 1930?" I asked the archivist.

She walks to the back room and brings out a large old book, dark brown, binded with cracks, and missing, illegible pages. It seemed so delicate and broken. With each flip of its pages, I wonder what secrets they hold and what they have witnessed in this room. I wonder how many lives were changed by simply seeing the names of their loved ones on these pages and soon I will too, *InshaAllah*[4].

Each page I turn, I scan the columns saying *Name of Infant,* hoping to see my Ma's name.

Two pages, ten pages, twenty pages, I flip through.

I gasp. *Subhan Allah*[5], I finally saw Bibi Nazmoon. I realize it was the first time I ever saw her name written down.

---

[2] Paternal brother
[3] Paternal mother
[4] Arabic phrase popularly used by Muslims that translates to "God willingly."
[5] Arabic phrase popularly used by Muslims that translates to "Praise be to God"

No.	Name of Infant.	Sex.	Race.	Date of Birth. (1930)	Description of Father		Description of Mother				Place of Birth	REMARKS.
					Name.	No.	Name.	No.	Name of Ship in which Introduced	Year of Arrival		
897	Bibi Nazmoon	F	Calcutta	3 June	Ameerally	213	Kariman	103827	Moy	1902	Rose hall	some illegible scratches

Immigration Ordinance.   **No. 18, 1891, Section 205.**

Register of Births Occurring Amongst the Immigrants Residing in the County of Berbice

Seeing the word *Rosehall* brings images of the resistance against British colonization led by Muslim indentured labourers in 1914 and how Kariman may have aided in organizing the rebellion. I wonder if she knew anyone murdered or if she was injured in the violent 1914 Rose Hall Massacre[6] at the hands of white British colonizers after the rebellion.

"What do these numbers mean?" I ask the archivist, pointing to the six digits (103827) near Kariman's name.

"It means that Kariman was not born in *British Guiana*. She was displaced on a ship, and from that number she was assigned, we can trace her *Girl's Emigration Pass*," says the archivist.

I could feel my heart beating faster and my eyes beginning to burn just thinking about how the moment of revelation is so close, so tangible. I could almost reach out and grab it.

---

[6] Apart of the intergenerational trauma Muslim Indo-Caribbeans experience is the Rose Hall Massacre, rooted in the colonial resistance of Muslim indentured "riot-leaders" including Aladi, her husband Chotey Khan and Amirbaksh (who were Indian Muslims) and Moula Bux, Jahangir Khan and Dildar Khan (who were Afghan Pathans), leading to the bloody violent murder of 15 people and 41 injured by evil white colonizers. For more information please refer to Karimah Rahman's article entitled "*Muslim Indo-Caribbean Identity: Muslim Indentured Resistance to Colonization and Colonial Policies*" published in 2020 by The Migration Initiative, https://www.themigrationinitiative.ca/post/the-influence-of-muslim-indentured-labourer-resistance-to-british-colonization-and-colonial-policies and Raymond S. Chickrie's article entitled "*The Afghan Muslims of Guyana and Suriname*" published in 2002 by the Journal of Muslim Minority Affairs and Bibi H. Khanam and Raymond S. Chickrie's article entitled "170th Anniversary of the Arrival of the First Hindustani Muslims from India to British Guiana" published in 2009 in the Journal of Muslim Minority Affairs.

The archivist emerges from the back room with a few large books in her hand. Knowing that somewhere in those pages contains some answers to many of my unanswered questions I had my whole life about where I come from was unbearable.

I flip through one book, no Kariman. Daddy and *Chacha* leaf through the book a second time as a precaution. I am so thankful for their help in getting me to the archives and the ability to share this moment with them. I can sense their excitement as well; in finally being able to uncover more about their *Nani*[7] whom they have such a deep love and respect for.

I take another book and start to flip through the pages gently so they don't rip. To think all they provide is hand sanitizer as a form of protection and preservation of these books is disheartening. Especially the condition these books are kept in, with such little precautions taken. Some pages are already missing and torn. The descendants of the indentured labourers listed will never know the knowledge contained about their ancestors hidden in those missing pages lost forever. I begin to worry if one of those pages might be my ancestors' Emigration Pass.

Two pages, ten pages, twenty pages, I flip through.

I keep repeating, "*Bismillah Hir Rahman Nir Raheem, Qul huwal lahu ahad, Allah hus-samad, Lam yalid walam yulad, Walam yakul-lahoo kufuwan ahad*[8]," and then blow on the book three times without the archivist looking.

Fifty pages, seventy-five pages, one hundred pages, one hundred twenty-five pages, I flip through.

---

[7] Maternal grandmother
[8] A popular *surah* or chapter in the *Qur'an* recited by Muslims.

My eyes scan the page and then my fingers begin trembling. *Allahu Akbar*[9]. It's her, Kariman. Internally, I wanted to collapse and cry uncontrollably as an emotional release, since today is the day I waited for my whole life. Everything I ever did to research the history of Muslim indentured labourers (especially Muslim Indo-Caribbeans in Trinidad and Guyana), to research my family ancestry, all the questions I asked all my family members, especially my elders, has lead up to this moment.

"Daddy, *Chacha*, I have your *Nani*'s Emigration Pass!" I yell.

They come over, eager to scan the page and together we unravel our history, never told before.[10]

Finally, I knew at least one tangible place I can touch on a map that I was originally from and where my ancestry lies. When I'm asked where in

---

[9] Phrase popularly used by Muslims that translates to God is most great from Arabic.

[10] The Moy ship docked on August 20th, 1902

South Asia or India I'm from, I have an actual location in India to say. It was as if the holes in my collective intergenerational memory were slowly being filled little by little. I waited my entire life to be able to experience this very special moment of knowing. This small simple page was the key that unlocked so many answers, and at the same time, raised so many questions on who my ancestors were and who I am.

Reading the word *Meerut* makes me think of the First War of Independence (problematically referred to as the Sepoy Rebellion) that began in Meerut due to the labour of dalit colonial resistance by freedom fighters like Matadin Bhangi (Valmiki), not upper caste Brahmin sepoys like Mangal Pandey. I wonder how my ancestors in colonized India resisted and fiercely fought white British colonizers during the First War of Independence. I wonder if any of my ancestors were forcefully displaced to the Caribbean as indentured labourers bounded to plantations as punishment for resisting British colonization like the freedom fighter Mazar Khan[11] (Pathan) from Meerut, who was forcibly displaced to *British Guiana*.

Under caste, *Musalman* is written, but that only refers to Kariman being Muslim, not her specific caste. Of course the white colonizers wouldn't know the difference. Those who have Hindu indentured ancestors have the ability to view their ancestors' caste on their Emigration Pass, it doesn't just state *Hindu* under caste like how the broad term *Musalman* was mainly written for Muslims. I know Muslims are separated in a caste-based hierarchy[12]

---

[11] For more information refer to Raymond S. Chickrie's article entitled "*The Afghan Muslims of Guyana and Suriname*" published in 2002 by the Journal of Muslim Minority Affairs.
[12] The caste-based hierarchy among Muslims in India (and the Indian Diaspora) is remodeled from the caste system in Hinduism with *varnas* (caste)

that is not rooted in Islamic theology, that is comprised of *Ashraf*[13] (upper

caste), *Ajlaf/Azlaf* (lower caste, shudra Muslims with Indian ancestry) and

Arzal (Dalit Muslims with Indian ancestry), with the overwhelming majority

of Muslims (75 %[14]) in India as *Arzal*/Dalit specifically (85%[15] of Muslims are

backward/oppressed pasmanda castes composed of both *Ajlaf/Azlaf* and

Arzal/Dalit). The overwhelming majority of displaced indentured labourers

in the Caribbean were not among those with the most power/privilege in

Hindostan[16], but rather many were among those vulnerable and marginalized

on the periphery. *Arzal*/Dalits would have formed a significant portion of

Muslims during indentureship. I know Muslim indentured labourers

displaced to the Caribbean are also comprised of scheduled tribes[17], Adivasis

and Indigenous communities as well.

Since my ancestor Kariman was Muslim, and an *Ashraf*/upper caste

like *Pathan*, *Sheik/Shaikh*, *Syed* or *Mughal* caste was not specified on her

Emigration Pass like on a few[18] of the other displaced Muslim indentured

---

[13]*Ashraf* are considered upper caste (foreign, noble, royalty or descending from the family of the Prophet PBUH) such as Sayyad/Syed, Sheikhs and Pathans, who can be viewed as the equivalent of Brahmins in the Hindu caste system. Each of the previous caste umbrella categories of *Ashraf*, *Ajlaf/Azlaf* and *Arzal* are intersectional categories composed of various sub-castes and positionalities as well. The previous information on castes among Muslim indentured labourers displaced to the Caribbea is from Karimah Rahman's article "*Who are Muslim Indo-Caribbeans?*" published by Brown Girl Diaries in 2020 https://www.browngirldiary.com/post/who-are-muslim-indo-caribbeans, please read for more information.

[14] For the percentage please refer to the article entitled "*Why are many Indian Muslims seen as untouchable?*" by Soutik Biswas and published in 2016 by BBC https://www.bbc.com/news/world-asia-india-36220329

[15] For the percentage please refer to the article entitled "*India's Muslim community under a churn: 85% backward Pasmandas up against 15% Ashrafs*" by Khalid Anis Ansari and published in 2019 by The Print https://theprint.in/opinion/indias-muslim-community-under-a-churn-85-backward-pasmandas-up-against-15-ashrafs/234599/

[16] Present day South Asia, former *British Raj* or colonial occupied pre-partition India

[17] Examples include Islamic names found among *Dhangur* indigenous peoples displaced to Guyana as indentured labourers. For more information refer to Bibi H. Khanam and Raymond S. Chickrie's article entitled "*170th anniversary of the arrival of the first hindustani muslims from india to british guiana*" published in 2009 by the Journal of Muslim Minority Affairs. This article also provides examples of castes among Muslim indentured labourers displaced to *British Guiana*.

[18] For more information refer to Bibi H. Khanam and Raymond S. Chickrie's article entitled "*170th anniversary of the arrival of the first hindustani muslims from india to british guiana*" published in 2009 by the Journal of Muslim Minority Affairs. This article provides examples of castes among displaced Muslim indentured labourers which include *Musulman/Mosulman/Musalman*, *Mahomedaan*, *Pathan/Pattian*, *Sheik/Shaikh*, *Syed*, *Jolaba* and *Mughal*. It is important to note that Muslim descendants

labourer's Emigration Passes, and since only *Musalman* was specified, she was most likely not an *Ashraf*/upper caste. I will never know what her exact caste was, but most likely she was a backward/oppressed pasmanda caste, either *Ajlaf*/*Azlaf* or *Arzal*/Dalit. I wonder what her family must have gone through living in *Hindostan* with systemic casteist and Anti-Pasmanda oppression. I wonder what Kariman's family/descendants are currently facing in India and how Kariman's circumstances may have changed (or were maintained) in different ways growing up in *British Guiana*[19].

"Why does it say Mo. Accomp. next to *'Name of Kin,'*" I ask the archivist.

"It means the mother accompanied the baby on the Moy ship. We can try to find her Emigration Pass as well," the archivist says.

I have the name of Kariman's father (Kurmobah), yet interestingly her mother, the woman who actually accompanied her on the ship, remains invisible and nameless on her Emigration Pass.

Growing up, the most precious information *Ma* told me was how her *Nani*[20] came to Guyana.

"*Deh white man ah trick she. Meh Nani nah know where dem been a tek she, she husband and she chirren,*" *Ma* would tell me. *Ma*'s *Nani* went to the Fyzabad depot with her husband and another daughter. They were all sent to Calcutta together, but at the Calcutta Port, when in the process of boarding the ship, her younger daughter saw jalebi selling so she ran to get

---

of indentured labourers may have lived experiences being marginalized (having casteist language used against them or their indentured ancestors), but simultaneously they have a positionality of power/privilege, since they do not have the lived experience of violent casteist/caste-based oppression in India (or among recent migrants) and they can not problematically self-identify as having the lived experience of their ancestors caste.

[19] *British Guiana* is the colonial term for present-day Guyana

[20] Maternal grandmother

some. *Nani*'s husband ran after the younger daughter and the boat started to leave before they could return onto the ship.

"Nani been ah cry for she bacha she whole life, she nah know where she deh. She even run in di water and try for swim back to India, thinking she go reach she village and she bacha. She never see she bacha or she family or she village or she beloved homeland again, and she die heartbroken never seeing am," *Ma* would tell me.

I frantically flip through the pages, hoping to see Kariman's mother's *Woman Emigration Pass.* I pray, *InshaAllah,* it wasn't one of the pages that was missing, crumbling, or illegible.

I flipped through ten pages, twenty pages, fifty pages, seventy-five pages, one hundred pages; the entire ship records and I still couldn't find her *Woman Emigration Pass.* My eyes are burning as I try to hold back the tears welling up so they don't fall on the ship records.

"Don't worry bacha, we will go through the ship records again," says Daddy.

"Nah worry. Meh go through am with you Daddy," says *Chacha.*

"Can I have a certified true copy of the Girl's Emigration Pass?" I ask the archivist.

"Are you looking to apply for the Overseas Citizenship of India (OCI) Card?" the archivist asks.

"Yes I am. Can I have three copies?" I ask.

"Yes, let me go to the back and get that for you.".

I was heartbroken. I never found Kariman's mother's *Women Emigration Pass,* but I was excited that I could apply for the OCI card. I could finally go to India[21] and know what it feels like to stand on my ancestral soil, to walk the same paths as my ancestors in my ancestral villages, and to hug tightly my family in India, *InshaAllah*. This is what I want more than anything else. Holding on to the thought of this makes up for not finding the Emigration Pass.

***

National Archives of Trinidad and Tobago (August 2018)

I always smile thinking of the family reunion I went to at Mayaro Beach; three generations of families all gathered together to celebrate their deceased *Nani*[22] and *Nana*[23]. Luckily, my *Khaala*[24] was able to get Shamshu Deen, a well-known genealogist in Trinidad, to trace our family's ancestry, but we never recovered my ancestor's Emigration Pass.

"*Mamee*[25] it's so cold in here," I say as I wait for the archivist at the National Archives of Trinidad and Tobago.

"Wuh is di name again and di ship and ting?" said *Mamu*[26].

"It's Khadimah. The ship is *Bruce* and the year it docked was 1860," I say.

"Looks like her pass should be in the General Register C- 1858-1906 (Registration Nos. 17270-17670) since that ship travelled from Madras and docked on the 6th of January, 1860. That is the only register we have with ships departing from Madras," says the archivist.

The archivist then rushes towards the backroom and finally emerges with what would be one of the most important documents I would ever come

---

[21] I acknowledge that the financial ability to even think of travelling to India as the descendant of indentured labourers is a privileged positionality.
[22] Maternal grandmother
[23] Maternal grandfather
[24] Maternal aunt
[25] Maternal uncle's wife
[26] Maternal uncle

across in my life. The heavy books filled with ship records were placed on the table and Mommy, *Mamu*, and *Mamee* help me comb through their pages.

We all silently recite *Qul huwal lahu ahad*[27] and blow on the pages as we flip through them.

Twenty-five pages, fifty pages, seventy-five pages, one hundred pages, one hundred twenty-five pages, one hundred fifty pages, we flip through.

SubhanAllah, my eyes finally meet Khadimah on the page and I find her Emigration Pass. Another ancestor I carry with me like Kariman, whom I am forced to learn about mainly through the crumbs left by white colonizers in the archives.[28]

Ship's Name ....Bruce.........
Ship's No. 489

La Plaisance

Trinidad Emigration Agency

25689

Madras, *the* ....23rd Sept, 1859

Depôt No. .... 1468 ....
Name .... Khadimah ....
Caste .... Musalman ....
Father's Name .... Kalim ....
Sex .... Female
Age .... 19 ....
Zillah .... Madura ....
Pergunnah .... Ramnad ....
Village .... Panaikulam ....
Occupation .... Laborer
Name of next-of-kin .... Raheemah Sis. ....
If married to whom, ... ------- ....
Bodily Marks .... 2-3 ....

Certified that I have examined and passed the above named as fit Subject for Emigration and that she is free from all bodily and mental disease — Having been Vaccinated.

Surgeon Superintendent

Depôt Surgeon.

I hereby certify that the woman above described (whom I have engaged as a labourer on the part of the Government of Trinidad where she has expressed a willingness to proceed to work for hire) has appeared before me and that I have explained to her all matters concerning her duties as an Emigrant".

Protector of Emigrants Madras.

Emigration Agent for Trinidad

---

[27] A popular *surah* or chapter in the *Qur'an* recited by Muslims.

[28] Later Emigration Passes included, *I hereby certify that the man/woman above described (whom I have engaged as a laborer on the part of the government of Trinidad where he/she has expressed a willingness to proceed to work for hire) has appeared before me and that I have explained to him/her all matters concerning his/her duties as an Emigrant, according to Section XXXVIII of Indian Emigration Act No. VII of 1871.*

Growing up, I was always told that I look Southern Indian or Sri Lankan, specifically Tamil and that I have Tamil features. The first thing I'm drawn to on the Emigration Pass is the district Khadimah is from. It is located in present-day Tamil Nadu, in the predominantly Tamil Muslim village of Panaikulam. This means Khadimah was Tamil, and she most likely spoke Tamil. Ever since I was young, I was always drawn to the beauty of the Tamil language, the fast tempo beats in Tamil *gaana* music and Tamil films (Kollywood). I always found comfort in Tamil people[29].

I always felt a strong connection to Tamil films growing up because I found something in them I couldn't receive from Bollywood movies. In Tamil films, for the first time, I saw a reflection of myself on screen. I experienced colourism/shadeism growing up, through bullying and microaggressions about my skin color being viewed externally as 'too dark,' 'not beautiful' and even 'ugly.' Despite this bullying, I was always proud of my dark skin and I saw the beauty in my melanin that others wouldn't due to white supremacy and a colonial mentality. When I watched Tamil films[30], it was the first time I saw some women that were not the status quo, light skinned Northern Indians I would stereotypically see in Bollywood films. I was able to see on screen some Southern Indian women with darker skin tones, whom I saw myself in more. Some of these women include Aishwarya

---

[29] This connection to Tamil people included having a shared lived experience with marginalization and '*othering*' within South Asian and Indian spaces that I also experience as an Indo-Caribbean. With that mutual understanding, I always found acceptance in Tamil spaces and I felt more seen, unlike in other South Asian and Indian spaces.

[30] This is not to say that colourism/shadeism isn't present in Southern Indian film industries, I acknowledge the widespread problematic preference for 'light/pale' skin and Northern Indian aesthetics in Kollywood. Just look at how white supremacy and colonialism is so internalized to the point that white people like Amy Jackson are cast as leads in Tamil films in what are meant to be ethnic Tamil roles, along with the lack of actual Tamil actresses (and Tamil-speaking actresses) who are ethnically Tamil and the rampant use of brown face (darkening of the skin tone for roles such as depicting villagers as well as dalits and reproducing Anti-Blackness) in the Tamil (and Southern Indian) film industry. Women with darker skin tones in Bollywood films are mainly Bengali like Kajol, Rani Mukerji, Konkana Sen Sharma and Bipasha Basu.

Rajesh (in *Rummy, Kaaka Muttai* and *Vada Chennai*), Parvathy Thiruvothu (in *Maryan/Mariyaan*) and Amala Paul (in *Velaiilla Pattadhari*), and Sai Dhanshika (in *Paradesi*). Watching the 2013 Tamil film *Maryan* (*Mariyaan*)[31] was the first time I saw my favourite actor, Dhanush, cast opposite someone who also had a darker skin complexion. When watching the 2013 Tamil film *Paradesi*, which explored the *kangani*[32] system, I finally felt seen. I saw similarities to what my ancestors experienced as displaced indentured labourers depicted on screen, their lived experiences of oppression, exploitation, violent physical torture and horrendous living conditions.

I still remember the first time I heard Tamil spoken in a film and sung in a song; the hairs on my body stood up and I felt a jolt like an electric shock. It was as if something deep, hidden in my DNA, was alive and finally waking up. Something that I was not conscious of previously. My DNA recognized the familiarity of the Tamil language to my ancestry and me, which the white colonizers tried so hard to erase. I knew that my ancestors were communicating within me, with each generation leaving traces of themselves, so that part of myself, body and blood, will still be connected to them and resonate with Tamil. It amazes me to this day that no other language compares to the pull I feel towards the Tamil language. This realization allowed experiences across my life to finally start making more sense. The only other languages I'd ever felt pulled towards was *Urdu* when sung in the knowledge production and form of colonial resistance of my ancestors that is *qaseedas/qasidas*[33] entrenched in my Muslim Indo-Caribbean childhood.

---

[31] It is important to note that the film *Maryan*(*Mariyaan*) problematically reproduces Anti-Black Racism and Anti-Black stereotypes.

[32] I acknowledge that the *kangani* system is different from the *indentureship* system, but they do share some similarities as both a form of colonial intergenerational trauma stemming from displacement and horrendous working conditions under the oppression of bondage.

[33] Religious songs of praise sung by Muslims, especially popular in South Asia as well as the South Asian diasporas.

Bhojpuri and *Awadhi* remnants from the ancestors oral traditions, and *Bangla*
(*Bengali*), a language heard by my ancestors displaced from the Calcutta port
and interestingly the background I'm sometimes guessed to have due to my
last name being *Rahman*.

I begin to wonder why Muslim Southern Indians (including Tamils)
are invizibilized, silenced, and marginalized in Indo-Caribbean, including
Muslim Indo-Caribbean spaces.

Like Kariman, Khadimah did not have an *Ashraf/*upper caste like
Pathan, *Sheik/Shaikh*, *Syed* or *Mughal* caste specified on her Emigration Pass
like on a few (10%[34]) of the other displaced Muslim indentured labourer's
Emigration Passes. Since only *Musalman* was specified, she was most likely
not an *Ashraf/*upper caste. Again, I will never know what her exact caste was,
but most likely she was a backward/oppressed pasmanda caste, either
Ajlaf/Azlaf or *Arzal/*Dalit. Like Kariman, I wonder what Khadimah's family
must of went through living in *Hindostan*[35] with systemic casteist as well as
Anti-Pasmanda oppression. I wonder what Khadimah's family/descendants
are currently facing in India and how Khadimah's circumstances may have
changed (or were maintained) in different ways growing up in *Chinidad*[36].

---

[34] In the case of Trinidad ,10% of Muslim indentured labourers that were displaced from 1887-1891 were listed on Emigration passes as "*Pathans*, *Sheiks/Shaikh* or *Syed*" etc., which happens to be *Ashraf/*upper castes, currently in India *Ashrafs* represent a minority percentage of 15% of Indian Muslims. Please refer to Halima-Sa'adia Kassim's 2020 lecture entitled "*Indentured Muslims in Trinidad*" for Indian Arrival Day by The Islamic Resource Society (IRS) & The Trinidad Muslim League (TML) https://www.researchgate.net/publication/342534278_Indentured_Muslims_in_Trinidad_-. For the percentage please refer to the article entitled "*India's Muslim community under a churn: 85% backward Pasmandas up against 15% Ashrafs*" by Khalid Anis Ansari and published in 2019 by The Print https://theprint.in/opinion/indias-muslim-community-under-a-churn-85-backward-pasmandas-up-against-15-ashrafs/234599/. This begs the question if the indentured labourers displaced who were listed as only *Musalman*(*Mosulman*) on the Emigration Passes were of *Azlaf/Ajlaf*(lower caste) or *Arzal*(dalit) Pasmanda Castes since Muslim indentured labourers who specified their caste self-identification were in fact upper caste (*Ashraf*) Muslims, who comprise similar minority percentage breakdowns currently in India.

[35] Present day South Asia, former *British Raj* or colonial occupied India

[36] *Chinidad* is a term for Trinidad used during colonization

With Khadimah assigned to the *La Plaisance* estate, I wonder if her or her descendants were involved in organizing or harmed in resisting against the white British colonizers in the Hosay Massacre of 1884[37].

"Why does it say Sis. next to 'Name *of next-of- kin*?'" I ask the archivist.

"It means that Khadimah was with her sister on the same ship and we can try to find her Emigration Pass as well," said the archivist.

I frantically flip through the pages, hoping I see Raheemah's *Woman Emigration Pass* and hoping it wasn't one of the pages that were lost, crumbling or illegible.

Ten pages, twenty pages, fifty pages, seventy-five pages, one hundred pages, I flip through. Eventually, I flipped through the entire ship records and I still couldn't find her Emigration Pass. I could feel my eyes burning trying to hold back tears.

"If Allah wills us to find it today we will. If not, doh worry we can try the next time we visit Trinidad,'" says Mommy, while holding me in her arms.

"Doh worry we go'in thru it with yuh Mummy," says *Mamu* and *Mamee.*

---

[37] After The Indian Festivals Ordinance of 1882 prohibited *Hosay* to be celebrated in the roadway, reports of 8-10 thousand (and up to 30,000 people) defied the Ordinance and held their *taziyas* in procession for *Hosay* leading to the violent Hosay Massacre in 1884 with 120 injured and 22 murdered by evil white British colonizers. This is apart of the intergenerational trauma Muslim Indo-Caribbeans experience and this colonial act of resistance by Muslim indentured labourers was supported in solidarity by non-Muslim participants like Afro-Caribbeans, Hindus and Christians, we need the energy of this solidarity in the present and future. For more information please refer to Karimah Rahman's article entitled "*Muslim Indo-Caribbean Identity: Muslim Indentured Resistance to Colonization and Colonial Policies*" published in 2020 by The Migration Initiative, https://www.themigrationinitiative.ca/post/the-influence-of-muslim-indentured-labourer-resistance-to-british-colonization-and-colonial-policies, the Caribbean Muslims article entitled "*The Hosay or Muharram Massacre of 1884 in Trinidad*" https://www.caribbeanmuslims.com/the-hosay-or-muharram-massacre-of-1884-in-trinidad/ and the Trinidad Daily Express Newspaper article entitled "*Remembering the 1884 Jahaji Massacre*" https://trinidadexpress.com/news/local/remembering-the-jahaji-massacre/article_c7769a29-752c-504f-95d4-65e983800034.html.

With a heavy heart, I never found Raheemah's *Women Emigration Pass.*

Khadimah and Raheemah grew up together in *Hindostan*, endured crossing the *kala pani*[38] together in horrendous conditions, only to be forcefully separated by these evil white colonizers. They were bound to different estates in Trinidad so their descendants would live apart, in the same country, and never know the other existed for generations. Somewhere in Trinidad is Raheemah's family, my family, and *InshaAllah,* one day I will find them.

We exit the archives and I sit in the back seat of my *Mamu*'s car. I stare outside the window at the familiar comforting sites of Trinidad while clutching Khadimah's Emigration Pass tightly.

I can't help but think about how Kariman and her mother were deceived by evil white British colonizers. There is oral knowledge passed down from our ancestors describing people being stolen from India to meet quotas for indentured labourers on ships; I wonder if any of my ancestors were ever stolen from their villages or deceived within the gamut of unfreedom and agency that is indentureship. I can't help but imagine the pain and trauma Kariman, her mother, Khadimah, Raheemah, and my other ancestors endured. They never knew they would be ripped away from their beloved homeland, their village, land, home and all they ever known to never see their family or *Hindostan's* shores ever again, due to the violent displacement of indentureship under British colonization. I think about how we need to radically unpack *Indentureship's Intersectional Intergenerational Trauma*, how we carry it in our cells and genes with each generation. How it is reproduced

---

[38] *Kala pani* is a term used to refer to 'black water' or seas indentured labourers crossed and the loss of their respectability as well as *varna* (caste), it should be noted that the *kala pani* however does not hold the same significance regarding caste for Muslim indentured labourers

in our day to day intersectional lived experiences and how it impacts mental health in the Indentured Diasporic and Indo-Caribbean community. I think about how problematic it is to celebrate the beginning of this horrific system of indentureship rooted in colonial violence, displacement and intergenerational trauma that is Indian Arrival Day (and South Asian Arrival Day in Canada). I think about how we must radically unpack and decolonize Indian Arrival Day (and South Asian Arrival Day) so we can continue our journey of decolonization by unlearning colonial harm and resisting this violent history and *Indentureship's Intersectional Intergenerational Trauma*. We must radically unpack and decolonize Mental Health in the Indentured Diasporic and Indo-Caribbean community rooted in the bounded system of indentureship.

My eyes burn with rage as I imagine the patriarchy, misogyny, physical, as well as sexual violence and rape, Kariman, her mother, Khadimah and Raheemah experienced under colonization. These womxn and children I never met, but love so deeply. I imagine how fearful it must have been to be so far away from everything familiar. But at the same time I think of how Muslim womxn indentured labourers in the Caribbean had such strength and were so fiercely unapologetic when resisting colonial oppression[39], patriarchy and

---

[39] Scholars like Raymond Chickrie praise the involvement of *Pathans* in acts of resistance to colonization in India as well as the Caribbean, please refer to Chickrie's article entitled *"The Afghan Muslims of Guyana and Suriname"* published in 2002 in the Journal of Muslim minority affairs. At the same time that we acknowledge Muslim voices in Indentured history, it is important to be critical of emphasizing Muslim upper caste/*Ashraf* (such as *Pathan*) narratives of resisting colonization as exemplary since all acts of colonial resistance are rooted in the labour and resistance of those most oppressed such as Muslim dalits/*Arzals*, scheduled tribes, Adivasis and other indigenous peoples especially queer, trans and womxn. Examples of *Pathan*-centric narratives of colonial resistance among Muslim indentured labourers in the Caribbean include Salamea, the Rose Hall Massacre riot-leaders Moula Bux, Jahangir Khan and Dildar Khan as well as Rogy (a Pathan *Mussulman* who resisted on the Non Pariel (Nonpariel) Plantation in 1896). For more information please refer to Rampersaud Tiwari's 2013 article entitled *"The October 1896 Non Pareil Uprising- The Unknown Story"* published in the journal *Man in India*. These examples are of how upper caste/*Ashraf*, specifically *Pathan* narratives dominate representations of Muslim Indo-Caribbean collective cultural history/memory in resistance against coloniazation in the Caribbean and Pathan-centric history/memory should not be the only narrative remembered.

misogyny, like Aladi[40], Salamea[41] (Pathan) or Tetary Begum Janey[42]. How

(*Radical*) *Muslim Indo-Caribbean Feminism* (*Muslim Indentured Diasporic*

Feminism) needs to be amplified rather than invizibilized, marginalized and

silenced in Indo-Caribbean (and Indentured Diasporic) spaces. I realize I am

the daughter of indenture, the strength of these past womxn (Kariman, her

mother, Khadimah, Raheemah) who have walked before me, who are my

ancestors. With each act of their resistance against colonization, energy, and

hope awakens inside me. These powerful womxn who survived, thrived, and

endured so many hardships under colonization are my source of strength and

make me who I am today. To know that this strength and resistance lies within

my blood allows me to know I can overcome future hardships.

     I feel more and more excited about finally going back home to India

and being able to step my foot on the same land that birthed these strong

womxn ancestors who embodied colonial resistance, which is what I want

more than anything else.

     "May I have a certified true copy of the Emigration Passes to use

when applying for the OCI," I ask the archivist.

     The archivist hands me a *Certified Copy of Record* form to fill out.

---

[40] For more information please refer to Karimah Rahman's article entitled "*Muslim Indo-Caribbean Identity: Muslim Indentured Resistance to Colonization and Colonial Policies*" published in 2020 by The Migration Initiative, https://www.themigrationinitiative.ca/post/the-influence-of-muslim-indentured-labourer-resistance-to-british-colonization-and-colonial-policies and Raymond S. Chickrie's article entitled "The Afghan Muslims of Guyana and Suriname" published in 2002 by the Journal of Muslim Minority Affairs and Bibi H. Khanam and Raymond S. Chickrie's article entitled "*170th Anniversary of the Arrival of the First Hindustani Muslims from India to British Guiana*" published in 2009 in the Journal of Muslim Minority Affairs.

[41] Salamea, a Muslim (Pathan) womxn indentured labourer played a key role in organizing and leding a strike/rebellion as an act of resistance against patriarchal colonization on the Friends Plantation in Berbice (*British Guiana*/Guyana) in 1903. For more information refer to Walter Rodney's 1981 article "*A history of the Guyanese working people, 1881-1905 (No. 988.1 R6)*", Rampersaud Tiwari's 2013 article entitled "*The October 1896 Non Pareil Uprising- The Unknown Story*" published in the journal *Man in India* and Aliyah Khan's, 2018 article entitled "*Protest and Punishment: Indo-Guyanese Women and Organized Labour*" published in the journal Caribbean Review of Gender Studies.

[42] For more information, refer to Usha Marhé's website article entitled "*Indian and Caribbean Diaspora*", https://ushamarhe.wordpress.com/about/roots-indian-diaspora/.

"Don't forget, the standard time for the certification of a record is three working days and your *Certified Copy of Record Form* must be completed," says the archivist.

***

Toronto - Canada (December 2019-March 2020)

"Shoot the Traitors": Uttar Pradesh sees the most deaths and violence in Anti-CAA protests[43].

    Twenty-three people murdered, mostly Muslims by police in Uttar Pradesh, one of the worst-hit states during Anti-CAA[44] (Citizenship Amendment Act)/NRC[45](National Register of Citizens) Protest Violence.

---

[43] These news headlines listed are inspired from real events during the Anti-CAA/NRC protests in India (especially in Uttar Pradesh and Tamil Nadu). For more information refer to: Prabhjit Singh's article *"A year on, no FIRs against Meerut police for men killed in CAA protests, PIL languishes in Allahabad HC"* published in 2020 in The Caravan https://caravanmagazine.in/crime/meerut-five-muslim-caa-protests-shot-police-families-allege, the Human Rights Watch 2020 article entitled *"Shoot the Traitors": Discrimination Against Muslims under India's New Citizenship Policy* https://www.hrw.org/node/340509/printable/print, The Indian Express 2019 article entitled *"UP sees most deaths and violence in anti-CAA protests: The stories we know so far"* https://indianexpress.com/article/india/uttar-pradesh-citizenship-law-protests-yogi-adityanath-6185483/. The Economic Times article published in 2019 entitled *"Internet suspended in 21 UP districts over Citizenship Amendment Act"* https://m.economictimes.com/news/politics-and-nation/internet-suspended-in-21-up-districts-over-citizenship-amendment-act/articleshow/72989827.cms, Scroll.in article entitled *"Citizenship Act: Internet suspended in several UP districts as state prepares for Friday protests"* https://scroll.in/latest/947986/citizenship-act-internet-suspended-in-several-up-districts-as-state-prepares-for-friday-protests and the Scroll.in article entitled *"CAA: Protests erupt across Tamil Nadu a day after Chennai Police baton charge demonstrators"* https://scroll.in/latest/953254/caa-protests-erupt-across-tamil-nadu-a-day-after-chennai-police-baton-charge-demonstrators.
[44] The CAA amends the Citizenship Act of 1955, so that naturalized Indian citizenship can be granted to migrants from Afghanistan, Pakistan, and Bangladesh who are of Hindu, Sikh, Buddhist, Jain, Parsi and Christian backgrounds. This option is NOT extended to Muslims. The CAA goes directly against Article 14 of the Indian Constitution by not providing the fundamental right of equality under the law, thus being illegal, undemocratic, against secularism, and unconstitutional. If the CAA was created under humanitarian reasons like what the BJP is suggesting then other minorities persecuted in surrounding countries should be included like Tamils from Sri Lanka, Buddhists from Tibet, Hindus from Bhutan, Christians from Nepal, Rohingya Hindus from Myanmar to name a few. (These arguments have been popularly cited in multiple sources, some sources include Anil Varughese's article entitled *"India's new citizenship act legalizes a Hindu nation"* published in 2019 in The Conversation https://theconversation.com/indias-new-citizenship-act-legalizes-a-hindu-nation-129024).
[45] The NRC calls for the register of all Indian citizens to be implemented across India by 2021, where each individual must prove Indian citizenship with ancestry documents. Assam has undergone this from 2013-2014. This process will be incredibly difficult, especially in rural areas where record-keeping is minimal, for precarious migrants and for those who do not have birth certificates or other official documents leaving many dalit, adivasi, scheduled tribe, indigenous especially disabled and trans communities vulnerable. (These arguments have been popularly cited in multiple sources, some sources

Five Muslim men murdered, shot and killed by police in Meerut on December 20th, 2020, the most intense burst of violence within two weeks of Anti-CAA/NRC protests.

Mobile and Internet services suspended Across UP including Meerut amid Anti-CAA protests.

Uttar Pradesh Police arrested 1,113 people in 327 cases registered and placed another 5,558 people under preventive detention during Anti-CAA and NRC protests.

Thousands of Muslims protest the CAA and NRC in the streets of Tamil Nadu.

Police lathi-charge Thousands of Anti-CAA/NRC Protesters, mainly Muslims in Tamil Nadu.

I could feel my heart beating faster with each article heading I read, especially since the CAA gained assent on December 12th, 2019 and came into force on January 10th, 2020. Coupled with the NRC, it has only led to the violent policing of protesters, mainly Muslims, who oppose these Anti-Muslim policies such as in Uttar Pradesh. I feel increased pain and fear for my family's safety back in India, especially in Uttar Pradesh[46] and Tamil Nadu after tracing my ancestors' Emigration Passes. The news article heading *Millions of Muslims in India Could End Up in BJP New Detention and Concentration Camps*[47] flashes across my Facebook and Instagram feeds.

---

includes the Human Rights Watch 2020 article entitled ""*Shoot the Traitors*": *Discrimination Against Muslims under India's New Citizenship Policy* https://www.hrw.org/node/340509/printable/print).

[46]A large portion of indentured labourer's ancestry can be traced to present-day Uttar Pradesh and a minority to Tamil Nadu.

[47] Those who do not make the NRC list and are Muslim will be sent to detention centers and concentrations camps, which are already under construction in Assam as well as other parts of India such as Punjab, Rajasthan, Maharashtra, Goa, Karnataka, New Delhi, and West Bengal. Under this planned genocide (such as the ongoing genocide in Assam) many migrants who were stripped of their citizenship are the very ones forced to construct these massive detention centers that will eventually 'incarcerate' these stateless people. (These arguments have been popularly cited in multiple sources, some sources include Bibhudatta Pradhan's article "*Millions in India Could End Up in Modi's New Detention Camps*" published in 2020 in Bloomberg https://www.bloomberg.com/features/2020-modi-india-detention-camps/

The proposed CAA and NRC policies combined together[48] leaves the citizenship of India's 200 million Muslims (who form 14%[49]of the population) across multiple generations questioned, and will render them stateless refugees imprisoned in detention centers and concentration camps across the country.

In February, article headings of Anti-Muslim violence continued.

Fifty-three people violently murdered and over 200 people injured in the Delhi 2020 Genocide, the Worst case of Anti-Muslim Violence in Decades[50]

---

and the DW article entitled "*India builds detention camps for Assam 'foreigners'*" https://www.dw.com/en/india-builds-detention-camps-for-assam-foreigners/a-50497835). It is important to note that this is all occurring within the context of an ongoing genocide in Kashmir. The research of Binish Ahmed in The Conversation 2019 article *Call the crime in Kashmir by its name: Ongoing genocide* (https://theconversation.com/call-the-crime-in-kashmir-by-its-name-ongoing-genocide-120412) furthers our understanding of the ongoing genocide in Kashmir as settler colonization as well as settler-occupation by the Indian state on the Indigenous Kashmiri peoples and their land.

[48] What cements the proposed CAA as being Anti-Muslim is when coupled with the NRC simultaneously. For example, the final updated Assam citizenship register left nearly 2 million people off the list with many living there for generations. A majority of those stripped of citizenship were Bengali Muslims, those remaining who were stripped of their citizenship and who were also not Muslim can now rely on the CAA. The CAA allows those not on the NRC to still obtain naturalized Indian citizenship and since those remaining stripped of citizenship are not Muslim and ONLY Muslims are specifically restricted from obtaining citizenship under the CAA, they are both Anti-Muslim policies. (These arguments have been popularly cited in multiple sources, some sources include The Guardian's 2019 article by Rebecca Ratcliffe and Kakoli Bhattacharya entitled "*India: almost 2m people left off Assam register of citizens*" https://www.theguardian.com/global-development/2019/aug/31/india-almost-2m-people-left-off-assam-register-of-citizens and the Human Rights Watch 2020 article entitled "*"Shoot the Traitors": Discrimination Against Muslims under India's New Citizenship Policy*" https://www.hrw.org/node/340509/printable/print).

[49] Muslims accounting for 14% of India or 200 million people were mentioned in Soumya Shankar's article entitled "*India's citizenship law, in tandem with national registry, could make BJP's discriminatory targeting of Muslims easier*" published in 2020 by The Intercept .

[50] These news headlines listed are inspired from real events during the Delhi 2020 genocide against Muslims.

For more information refer to: The Guardian 2020 article entitled "*Inside Delhi: beaten, lynched and burnt alive*" https://www.theguardian.com/world/2020/mar/01/india-delhi-after-hindu-mob-riot-religious-hatred-nationalists, The Human Rights Watch pdf document published in 2020 entitled "*"Shoot the Traitors" Discrimination Against Muslims under India's New Citizenship Policy*" https://www.hrw.org/sites/default/files/report_pdf/india0420_web_0.pdf, Shiv Sahay Singh's article entitled "*Delhi violence was a planned genocide, says Mamata Banerjee*" published in 2020 in The Hindu https://www.thehindu.com/news/national/other-states/delhi-violence-was-a-planned-genocide-says-mamata/article30961965.ece, Syed Khalique Ahmed's article entitled "*16 Mosques Destroyed By Mobs During Anti-Muslim Violence In Northeast Delhi: Delhi Minorities Commission Report*" published in 2020 in India Tomorrow https://old.indiatomorrow.net/eng/11-mosques-destroyed-by-mobs-during-anti-muslim-violence-in-northeast-delhi-delhi-minority-commission-report, Arpita De's article entitled "*A Delhi Neighbourhood Caught in the Riots Mourns the Death of Two Brothers*" published in 2020 by VICE https://www.vice.com/en/article/884dmp/two-brothers-killed-in-northeast-delhi-riots and Scroll.in Article entitled "*Delhi violence: 11 accused in killing of Muslim brothers worked with 'mob mind', says court*" published in 2020

Muslims Beaten, Lynched, Acid Attacked and Burnt Alive by Delhi's Hindu Supremacist Mobs.

Muslims Flee Their Homes and are Murdered in the Streets of Delhi by BJP Hindutva- supporting Mobs.

Eighteen Muslim Religious Places (Including Muslim Homes and Buisnesses) and Qur'ans Burnt and Petrol/LPG Cylinder Bombed in Delhi By Hindutva Mobs who Planted Saffron Flags on top Minarets of Masjids While Shouting "Jai Shri Ram", While Hindu Religious Places are Guarded and Protected by Local Muslims.

After Calling their Mother Minutes from Home, Two Muslim Brothers are Murdered and Later Fished out of the Drain among Nine others in Delhi.

Within this context of the CAA, NRC, Detention Centers and Concentration Camps, Anti-Muslim violence culminated in the Delhi 2020 genocide.

Then came the Coronavirus pandemic.

Indian Muslims Beaten and Blamed for Surge in CoronaVirus Infections[51]

#CoronaJihad: BJP use Coronavirus to stir-up Anti-Muslim Racism in India.

---

https://scroll.in/latest/968222/delhi-violence-11-accused-in-killing-of-muslim-brothers-worked-with-mob-mind-says-court,

[51] These news headlines listed are inspired from real events of Anti-Muslim Racism against Muslims in India during the Corona-19 Virus. For more information refer to: Aniruddha Ghosal, Sheikh Saaliq and Emily Schmall's article entitled *"Indian Muslims face stigma, blame for surge in infections"* published in 2020 on Toronto CityNews,
https://toronto.citynews.ca/2020/04/25/indian-muslims-face-stigma-blame-for-surge-in-infections/,
Joanna Slater and Niha Masih's article entitled *"As the world looks for coronavirus scapegoats, Muslims are blamed in India"* published in 2020 in The Washington Post
https://www.washingtonpost.com/world/asia_pacific/as-world-looks-for-coronavirus-scapegoats-india-pins-blame-on-muslims/2020/04/22/3cb43430-7f3f-11ea-84c2-0792d8591911_story.html and Siddharthya Roy's article entitled *"Hate Goes Viral in India: Anti-Muslim mudslinging has hit new heights as pandemic panic paves new avenues in India"* published in 2020 in The Diplomat https://thediplomat.com/2020/05/hate-goes-viral-in-india/

Over the past few months, especially since December 2019, the more article headings I read, the more violence and oppression Muslims continue to experience in India. They continue to experience Anti-Muslim oppression and violence when used as scapegoats and blamed for COVID-19.

The more I think about what is happening, the more it pains me that I do not know, or have a way of knowing, if my family in India is safe or still alive. I do not know what they are enduring with ongoing Anti-Muslim violence under the *Hindutva* ideology of the *Bharatiya Janata Party* (BJP)'s Hindu and Brahmin supremacist government under Modi. I find myself keeping track of updates on Anti-Muslim violence in India, especially in Meerut and Ramanathapuram, so I can piece together what is happening and imagine how my family may be affected. I find myself constantly fearful for this family I never met, wondering if they were harmed during the various Anti-CAA/NRC protests and if in their rural villages they have access to the 'proper' documentation required under the NRC. I am fearful that their citizenship will be stripped, or worse, if they will be sent to detention centers/concentration camps and what violence they're experiencing during the COVID-19 pandemic.

I sit on my *janamaz*[52] raising my hands to make *dua*[53] with tears streaming down my face for the safety of this family I do not know, I have never met, yet I have such deep love for, in India from afar. As I make *dua,* I realize even though I do not know who my exact family are in India, Allah knows exactly who each of my family members are, is watching over them and can send my love. This gives me some sense of comfort.

---

[52] Prayer mat used by Muslims to pray (*namaz*)

[53] dua literally means invocation, it is an act of supplication. The term is derived from an Arabic word meaning to 'call out' or to 'summon', and Muslims regard this as a profound act of worship. This is when Muslims connect with God and ask him for forgiveness and favors.

I lay on my bed, eyes pressed together, thinking about the Anti-Muslim political context with the BJP's *Hindutva*, Hindu and Brahmin supremacist government in India. I realize Muslims who resided in India for generations are having their citizenship stripped from them. The chances of me as a Muslim descendant of *Musalman* indentured labourers, displaced for generations before partition, to successfully obtain an Overseas Citizenship of India (OCI) Card or even a Visa to enter India for that matter may be slim[54]. I remember when filling out a Visa application form for India that the religion of parents and grandparents are collected, which is concerning being Muslim[55]. Knowing that Muslims are constantly policed as a '*dangerous security threat*' whose 'loyalty' must be questioned to India and are viewed as '*foreign/alien*' to India under *Hindutva* and Hindu supremacist rhetoric, this political context will naturally influence OCI and Visa application decisions under Modi's BJP government. These realizations fill me with dread as I realize I may not be able to visit the homeland of my traced ancestors in India; that I waited for my entire life and wanted nothing more to do with this Anti-Muslim political context and government.

As long as I can remember, I have always had a strong connection to my South Asian, especially Indian, heritage and identity growing up. I view South Asia, especially India, as *my* homeland, which is where my ancestors originated from before being deceived and displaced during violent colonization. Since I traced *my* ancestry from those two Emigration Passes, going to India was all I could think of. It was the moment I wished, dreamed,

---

[54] Especially with me being vocal against Anti-Muslim Racism and violence in India and the Indentured Diaspora (including Indo-Caribbean Diaspora) rooted in *Hindutva* ideology, Hindu and Brahmin supremacy.
[55] Especially if all these family members are Muslim as well or if you have what is deemed a 'Muslim sounding name.'

and prayed for the most ever since I could remember myself and all I ever truly wanted especially after already visiting my beloved Trinidad and Guyana.

As I gaze up at my Taj Mahal poster and map of India on the wall beside my bed, sandwiched between flags and maps of Trinidad and Guyana, I fight back tears at the thought that I may never be able to go to India and complete my journey back to *my* homeland, *my* home. I may never be able to walk on the shores of *my* homeland or have my feet step on *my* ancestral soil. As hot tears run down my cheek, I think I may never know how the land I came to love my whole life would feel under my feet, or know how it would feel the first moment I laid my eyes on its shores. I may never smell the natural sweet musk of *my* homeland and I may never see the ancestral homes or lands *my* ancestors previously lived on.

I start to wipe the tears as they reach my chin while I think. I may never know how it feels to have my forehead touch the ground of *my* homeland in *sujood*[56] while performing *namaz*[57]. I would never know how it would feel to hear the *adhan*[58], or go to *jummah*[59], or hear the *khutba*[60] in my native tongue, in *my* native land, in *my* ancestral village or family *masjid*[61]. The *masjid* my ancestors have gone to for generations before they were deceived and ripped from their homelands, displaced as indentured labourers in Trinidad and Guyana. The tears flow like a monsoon I will never see.

What pains me the most is that I am physically separated from my family in India. My family whom I will never know the feeling of meeting.

---

[56] the act of low bowing or prostration to God towards the direction of the *Kaaba* in *Mecca*

[57] *Namaz* is a Persian word used among the speakers of Persian, Turkish and among Muslims in South Asia when referring to the Islamic prayer known as *Salah/Salat* in Arabic. *Namaz* literally means 'prostration' and is used to mean 'prayer'.

[58] The *adhan*, also written as *adhaan, azan, azaan,* or *athan*, also called *ezan* in Turkish, it is the Islamic call to prayer, recited by the *muezzin* at prescribed times of the day. The root of the word is *'adhina* meaning 'to listen, to hear, be informed about'

[59] Friday midday congregational prayer

[60] a sermon preached in a *masjid/mosque* at the time of the Friday midday prayer

[61] Muslim place of worship also referred to as *mosque*

This family I speak of consists of the descendants of all my ancestors who had their family ties severed due to evil white British colonizers under the colonial violence of indentureship. I start to whimper, painfully thinking that I may never know what it would feel like the moment I see my blood in front of me, *my* family, or the moment I first embrace them and can transfer all the love I held for them in my heart all my life through a warm hug. I may never be able to get to know them, but knowing there is shared blood running through our veins, I still know we are forever connected although physically apart. I may never be able to even give my indentured ancestors the gift and comfort through me, so that they may know I saw and embraced their descendants and that all families once separated were finally reunited as one, as they should be. That the evils of colonial displacement could not keep us apart from each other in the radical resistance of reunification to be whole even after being displaced for generations. I may be here in Canada, but I was born with part of my heart in India, and it will forever remain there amongst my family, even if I may never lay my eyes upon them.

I think about how different the positionality of Hindu descendants[62] indentured labourers are; not needing to worry about being rejected to enter India if they wish to reconnect with family or visit their ancestral villages on the basis of their religion. Hindu Indo-Caribbeans (and Hindus in other indentured diasporas) have the power/privilege of greater accessibility[63] to enter India's borders and move about without needing to be cautious of Anti-Muslim Racism as well as violence.

This reality is a lot to take in; knowing *my* Muslim identity may become a barrier for me to physically enter India, visit *my* family, and step foot

---

[62] Especially Hindu descendants (and their family) who have what are deemed 'Hindu sounding names'
[63] I am referring to greater accessibility in regards to entry into India when one has the financial means to travel there and I acknowledge having the financial means to travel there is a power/privilege.

in *my* ancestral villages. This is because to be Muslim in Indian spaces (or the Indian Diaspora) is to be viewed as *'impure,' 'polluted,' 'inauthentic,' 'bastardized'* Indians who are *'foreign/alien,' 'dangerous,'* and a *'security threat,'* who's 'loyalty' must be questioned to India (and the Indian Diaspora)[64].

With all these realizations, I also recognize that as a Muslim descendant of *Musalman* indentured labourers, displaced to the Caribbean hailing from regions affected by the CAA as well as the proposed India-wide NRC, I am heartbroken over the treatment of Muslims in India. Although I have an emotional response to these Anti-Muslim policies, violence and accessibility issues to entering India to go to *my* ancestral village or to see *my* family, I must also acknowledge my power/privilege in this moment. The reality is that, as a descendant of indentured labourers born in Canada, I have accumulated power and privilege over time in regards to my Canadian citizenship[65]. I do not have the lived experience of being in India during various genocides against Muslims, experiences with violence surrounding the CAA and NRC, and my direct relatives in the Caribbean and 'the West' are not affected. Although I have lived experiences being oppressed and marginalized with Hindu purity politics, including *Hindutva* ideology, Hindu supremacy, and Anti-Muslim Racism in various spaces (such as Indian,

---

[64] For more information please refer to Karimah Rahman's article "*Muslim Indo-Caribbean Marginalization: In Indo-Caribbean, Indentured Diasporic, Caribbean, West Indian, Indian, South Asian and Muslim Spaces*" published in Brown Girl Diaries, https://www.browngirldiary.com/post/muslim-indo-caribbean-marginalization.
[65] My extended family has power/privilege due to their citizenship in Trinidad and Guyana, where our ancestors were displaced to during indentureship. Due to a second migration, I have citizenship in Canada (as well as my family), in relation to the precarious, violent and deadly lived experiences of Muslims in India regarding citizenship, thus giving me power/privilege.

Indentured diasporic, and Indo-Caribbean contexts[66]), I still have power/privilege since I am not experiencing this violence within the context of India. If my ancestors Kariman, her mother, Khadimah and Raheemah never boarded the Moy and Bruce ships, then my lived reality today would have been very different. If they were never displaced and never experienced the trauma of indentureship, my family would have still been in India. Most likely living in our rural villages, experiencing not only Anti-Muslim violence, but violence most likely coupled with casteist and patriarchal, misogynistic, sexist oppression. The reality is that with each breath I take here in Canada, knowing the security, power, and privilege I possess due to my citizenship, *my* family in India are being questioned of their citizenship and having to prove theirs.

South Asia and India are not something in my past, or something my ancestors left that is solely linked to history that ends the moment they boarded those ships; instead, it is a place that constantly dwells in my heart and in my present.

The biggest heartbreak of my life is to never be able to go back to *my* homeland, India. Even though I can not physically visit *my* homeland, I keep India and *my* ancestors alive each time I practice and remember *my* culture and *my* religion. I view this as *my* act of resistance against the violent colonization and displacement my ancestors endured during indentureship.

I WILL NOT FORGET!

---

[66] Hindu supremacy, Hindutva ideology, and Anti-Muslim Racism are reproduced in the Indentured Diaspora (among the descendants of indentured labourers or Indentured Diasporic spaces) as well as in the Indo-Caribbean Diaspora ,including policy due to Hindu Indentured Diasporic Supremacy, Hindu Indo-Caribbean Supremacy, Hindu Indentured Diasporic Privilege and Hindu Indo-Caribbean Privilege. For more information please refer to Karimah Rahman's article "*Muslim Indo-Caribbean Marginalization: In Indo-Caribbean, Indentured Diasporic, Caribbean, West Indian, Indian, South Asian and Muslim Spaces*" published in Brown Girl Diaries, https://www.browngirldiary.com/post/muslim-indo-caribbean-marginalization.

I am reminded of a line in the *qaseeda/qasida*, *Lap Pe Aati Hai Dua* that was my mother's signature song she was popularly known for singing in family and religious gatherings, *Ho mere dam se yunhi mere watan ki zeenat* (loosely translates to may my homeland through me attain elegance). Although I may never physically visit India, I vow to continue my process of constant decolonization, by resisting colonization while honouring the legacy of my *Musalman* indentured ancestors and the elegance of their homeland, by unlearning colonial harm, and learning to heal from my intergenerational trauma so that I may be unapologetically me today. So I may unapologetically call myself a Muslim, Indian, Indo-Caribbean, Trinidadian and Guyanese descendant of colonially displaced *Musalman* indentured labourers from present-day India, due to their sacrifices, strength, labour, survival and colonial resistance that allows me to thrive. We as a collective community of indentured labourer descendants were born and nurtured from their greatness.

As I lay on my bed, gazing up at the Emigration Passes on my wall, they serve as a constant reminder; the last thing I see before I go to bed, and the first thing I see when I wake up. I will never forget my indentured ancestors; their strength, their colonial resistance and where they come from— where *I* come from. Even if I may never be able to go home.

Wedding House

Alya Somar

I should have heard the muted and panicked whispers that evening when I was wrapping my hair in my towel. I should have felt the new weight in the air the moment I stepped out of the steamy bathroom. I should have noticed that the place cards for the reception were all forgotten and lacked the glitter that we added earlier. When I walked into the kitchen, it seemed like the heat of the stove had turned the room chilly.

The smell of turmeric in the air settled on top of our shoulders as the dahl cooled on the counter. There were forgotten bowls of bora that were half chopped on the cramped kitchen table. Auntie Reenie was sitting at the table with Joy, both of their arms crossed. When I entered, Joy looked up at me with her forehead creased. Aunty Reenie closed her eyes and inhaled. Aunty Ru and Rebecca were missing all together.

"What's wrong?" I asked.

Aunty Reenie's eyes were still closed. "Eden, sit down."

I stayed standing and raised my voice. "Why, what's happening?"

Joy stood up and grabbed me by the shoulders. I tensed at first, but folded when she sat me down in her chair.

"Is anyone gonna tell me what the hell is going on?"

"It's your mother," Aunty Reenie spoke over me. She looked me in the eyes with her chin up and her jaw set. "She's arriving tomorrow morning in time for the wedding."

My ears started to ring as my eyebrows arched up. I racked my brain for the right thing to say, or rather, I racked my brain for the right person to cuss. Mom, God, maybe Aunty Reenie herself told her? My finger shot up as I opened my mouth.

"We don't know," Joy said as she leaned against the fridge, her head in her hands.

I slammed my hand down and tried to speak again.

"Eden, don't act so surprised," said Aunty Reenie. "Did you really think you could keep this from your mother? Invite your whole family, invite her own mother; what did you expect to happen?"

"I expected people to have my back," I said.

Joy tried to reason with me, "We did. We kept our mouths shut. You know I haven't spoken to her since she left, same way as you."

I was up on my feet by then, my towel gone and my damp hair resting on my shoulders. Joy moved out of the way as I pulled out a cream soda from the fridge.

"Okay, fine, so it wasn't Joy." I turned back to the table and threw the cap on it. "So who was it then? Aunty Ru? Where is she?" I took a long swig.

Aunty Reenie rolled her eyes and put her hands on the table. "She went to the corner store with Rebecca to grab oil. Your Mom called after she left."

"So, she's out getting some air," I said. "What a nice idea!"

I slammed my drink on the table and grabbed Joy's hoodie from the banister. I snatched my keys from the bowl by the door and was out.

***

I left the house and headed down to Trinity Bellwoods. It was only a fifteen-minute walk from the house. It could have been pretty with the fading light and rustling leaves under different circumstances. That evening, the air was heavy, but the breeze kept it from standing still. The mugginess swirled around my thoughts. I felt the summer grime clinging to my skin again. I walked from one end of the park to the other for a good twenty minutes. Everyone was blowing up my phone, but I couldn't care less. I told Joy I was fine and that I wouldn't be long. My feet flew up and down the concrete. Next thing I knew, I was sitting in the grass, trying to think of a plan.

I could ask security to keep an eye out for her, that was supposed to be plan B. But then, what would I ask them to do when she showed up? Throw her out? Deny her entry? That would just create more problems for me. I felt like I was ten again. Once again, she had me where she wanted me and I would end up giving in and making things work for her. I had forgotten how exhausting it was. It made my head spin in circles. I had planned for every factor I could think of, but she was a wild card. Simply giving her radio silence wasn't enough to keep her away and I should have known that. I didn't want to ask her sisters to talk her out of showing up, but it seemed like my only option.

I felt the grass beneath me tickle my legs. It was the only thing keeping my head on the ground and not floating up into the clouds. My body grew hot from the building tension. I figured I'd have a few panic attacks the week of my wedding, I just didn't think that Mom would be the reason. Everyone promised they would keep their mouths shut so that she wouldn't be an issue. I started breathing like I had just sprinted down the aisle. I put my head in my hands and pulled my hair.

"Why are you sitting on the dutty ground?" Joy asked as she sat down in front of me. She loosened my fingers, taking them out of my hair and holding them in my lap. I didn't look up.

"I got tired," I mumbled.

"Of?" she asked.

I looked her in the eye.

"Being tired."

We sat like that for what felt like forever. We just stared at each other. I knew I looked angry, my entire face was tense. I could hear the blood rushing through my ears. After what felt like hours, Joy brought her own hands to her face and shut her eyes. She heaved a sigh that turned into a shuddering breath. She sniffled. She wiped both her eyes with the back of her hands.

"You know, some days I feel bad for her," Joy said.

"How?" I asked.

"Something must have gone wrong for her to do us so dirty."

"Uh, yeah. Something did go wrong. She flew off to the other side of the country when we were barely out of high school. Before that, she had her sisters teaching us how to take care of ourselves, and before that, she pawned us off on her mother—"

Joy rolled her eyes and cut me off. "No, I mean in order for her to pull that shit. I wanna know what must have happened to her. It's not normal."

"Mom's never been normal," I scoffed.

"There has to be a deeper reason, Eden."

"I get it. You want fi sympathize wit her. She's our mother for Christ's sake. Poor ting didn't get invited to her daughter's wedding. But just because we want to have some justification for what she's put us through, doesn't mean—"

"Auntie Reenie said in the kitchen yesterday that Mom wept at your baptism because she was scared God couldn't protect you... Same way he failed to protect her," Joy told me.

It was my turn to roll my eyes. "Maybe I wouldn't need God to protect me if I had my own mother."

"I'm sure Mom said the same thing about Granny.'

"So what, we all have Mommy issues? Love that for us."

Joy kissed her teeth and ripped the grass out of the ground. She took a deep breath before carrying on.

"We really all do. You know that. That's why I don't understand why you're being so goddamn extra about it now. I know you're mad about the past. I know you're scared about the future. But I don't see you trying to do anything about it right now."

Snot started running down my nose. My ears and neck got hot.

"Breathe, Eden."

I opened my mouth and a sob came out. My hands flew into my hair again until Joy grabbed me by the wrists. All I could do was kneel over and cry.

A few minutes after I had gotten my breathing under control for the second time, I sat hugging my knees to my chest.

"I wish we were all kids again, fighting over tamarind balls at Granny's house," I sniffed.

"Fi wah? So she could lash us top our heads and tell us to eat karela instead?" Joy joked.

"At least then we had someone making the decisions for us. This being grown thing sucks and we've been doing it for a long time. Do you think her pot spoon discipline is why I'm like this?"

"I think Granny's child rearing could be why Mom's the way she is. Then again, Mom raised us into the monsters we are today, so I guess yes?"

"Granny never bailed on us though," I said.

Joy got serious. "That's not the point I'm trying to make. What I'm saying is that the things Mom went through comes back to us."

"How so?" I asked.

"You think a normal Mom would bail on her kids the moment one started university if she hadn't gone through some hardships?"

"Facts."

"That's why I said I almost feel bad for her at times. Almost. I'm always going to be pissed about everything she didn't do for us, but I want to try to remember that she's a person like me and you all the same."

I still felt skeptical. "So, boo-hoo, the woman has feelings? Me too, she's not special."

Joy wasn't having it. "I'm saying she has some big feelings. We went through the Canadian-afied version of that stuff. Mom got the back-home version. Feel me?"

"Yeah," I nodded and looked Joy in the eye. "I think I do. We've heard the whisperings about Grandpa Peter. I don't think alcoholism could have made it any better."

"That's what I'm trying to say!" Joy was getting excited, talking with wild gestures. "It's the same story from all over the West Indies. Husband is a piece of work, wife takes the brunt of it and tries to do right by the kids. The family immigrated North and tries to pretend that their shit doesn't stink."

"The Immigrant Story," I say plainly.

"It's our Immigrant Story," Joy repeats.

"We were born here."

Joy's voice got quiet. "But we were raised like we were there."

"Everyone gets their ass beat with a pot spoon, how come they're not all like me?"

"Not true, those white kids from Church always had it good. Time outs and shit."

I smiled. "Imagine having parents that take away the T.V. remote and hug you when they do it."

Joy smiled. "What a life. Not a life for West Indians I guess."

"It really feels that way," I paused. "It's not just us and ours. It's Meena them, down the road. Uncle Simon and his wife back home. Your ex, Biggs, and his brothers—their shit followed them all the way out to Banff."

"It feels like a chronic disease. No matter how hard you try to shake it—"

"—it keeps hanging on."

The breeze started to feel even chillier with the sun gone. It cooled me down. I stretched my legs out on top of Joy's and she rubbed them. "You know how Mom talks bare shit about our Dad?" I asked.

"'The Sperm Donor,' yes. What about it?"

"What if he wasn't the problem."

Joy chuckled. "Oh honey, we've known."

I laughed. "Okay sure, but like, see the way Mom treats her kids? Imagine the way she must have treated her man!"

Joy started to giggle with me. "True, she's flighty as hell. Imagine trying to wife her."

We doubled over at Mom's expense. We stayed like that for a good while until we started to freeze our asses off.

"Joy."

"Eden."

"You laugh like a banshee," I chuckled.

"Imagine not being a bitch. What a concept."

I kicked Joy. She caught my leg and slapped it. We laughed even harder.

"I'm hungry, still." Joy was a lot of things, and famished was always one of them.

"Bang?"

"Bang."

So, we made our way to Bang Bang's.

***

The thing that no one tells you about crying is how hungry it can make you. Not always for a hot meal, but sometimes hungry for a friend. Or for a good book. Maybe a melodramatic album or two. Anything that can take your crying and put your revelations into words. That night for me, it was a frozen dairy-based treat. We shivered under the street lights as we ate our ice cream on the way home. The breeze died down, but it was still surprisingly cold for a July night. I had gotten a scoop of Lychee Rosewater and Joy got a scoop of London Fog.

"You eat like a swinge up old white lady," I poked at her.

"You eat like a Toronto hipster that gets married to a white guy who majored in philosophy."

"You didn't tell a lie." She didn't tell a lie.

We took the long way home and meandered through the neighbourhood. Wandering the street at night was something we had done growing up to pass the time when neither of us felt like going to bed in an empty house. The streets hadn't changed in the slightest since we were kids. I didn't mind it so much. Surprises are clearly not my thing. I liked knowing what to expect and how to expect it. Joy on the other hand, had a million plans on what she wanted to see from the neighborhood in the future. Facelifts on the houses, side streets without potholes, and a new fusion restaurant every two blocks. She believed it could be something great. At least great to her.

Joy brought me back to Earth when she asked, "Did you hear Rebecca tried to run away from home in February?"

My mouth flew open. "Sorry?"

"Yup. Something about it being her way of taking power away from her tyrannical father."

"I know those weren't Aunty Reenie's words."

"No, they're not. They're Becca's," Joy said.

"I didn't know you guys were close."

"I think she saw that I was the only adult cousin who didn't hide my alcohol in a red cup when she came to town, so I guess I'm cool or something."

"Well, congrats on being the cool cousin. Meanwhile I'm the one signing my life away to a white man and upholding the patriarchy," I laugh.

"She thinks you're alright."

Joy didn't need to lie to me. "She's twelve, yet the little anarchist flat out tried to dip and fend for herself. She saw she didn't like the way things were moving and she did something about it. She might be my hero," I said.

"I feel the same way." Joy smiled with pride. "The kid's got guts. Was it a terrible plan doomed for failure and ridicule the moment she leapt through her window? Yes. Did she give a fuck? No."

"That kid's going places."

"She reminds me of you."

I stopped in my tracks. "I shut up, sit down and do what I'm told. How is she anything like me?"

Joy smiled and rolled her eyes. "I'm serious. Whenever something needs to get done, you make it happen. She's the same way. She saw that her parents ain't shit and she tried to make something happen."

"What do I try to make happen?"

"See that crack in the concrete?" Joy nodded at the ground.

I looked down. "Yeah."

"That's how close you got to not having your own mother come to your wedding. Let me emphasize, your Guyanese mother who speaks to her sisters, that have raised you, daily. There were a thousand ways for things to go wrong earlier in the game, but still you had them go your way."

"I mean, she's still coming."

Joy huffed and started walking again. "Okay so she's showing up to the wedding. The wedding that you planned without her. The wedding that you paid for, without her. The wedding to the boyfriend you hid from her for six years."

"Okay, maybe I did a little something," I admitted.

"You did a lot of something, Eden. Say it with your chest."

We came up to the front of the house where Aunty Ru was on the phone with our Mom and smoking a cigarette. She waved at us as we approached.

"You know you can't outrun her, right?" Joy looked at me.

"Yes."

"So, what are you gonna do?"

"I don't know."

Glossary

Ajee: Paternal grandmother

Bacha: Child

Bacchanal: A term used to refer to drama or having a good time

Baigan Choka: Roasted, seasoned and mashed eggplant

Bajans: Devotional song with religious theme or spiritual ideas

Bhaji: Spinach

Bindi: Decoration worn on the forehead

Chacha: Father's brother

Chutney: A music genre created by East Indians with roots in Bhojpuri folk songs

Cook-up: Traditional one-pot Guyanese rice dish

Coolie: A low-wage laborer, typically of Asian descent

Creole: Language representing the Caribbean's hybrid cultures

Cutlass: A large flat bladed knife

Desi: People, cultures, and products of the Indian subcontinent and their diaspora

Diyas: Earthen oil lamp

Dhal: Split peas cooked until softened and thick

Dhal Puri: Indian Flat bread stuffed with seasoned split peas

Dhantal: Musical instrument

Dholak: Two-headed hand drum

Diwali: Hindu festival of lights

Dupatta: Shawl-like scarf traditionally worn by women

Filmi: Music from an Indian movie

Fete: Large parties

Geera: Roasted and ground cumin seeds

Ghungroos: A musical anklet tied to the feet of classical Indian dancers

Indenture: After the abolition of slavery in the Caribbean, the British brought Indians under contracts to work the plantations

Jalebi: Deep fried mixture of flour, sugar, milk
Jumbie: Spirit of a dead person, typically an evil one

Kala Pani: Indian ocean or "Dark Waters"

Karela: Popular vegetable in many Asian countries

Kurta: Indian wear for the upper half of the body

Lehenga: A form of ankle-length skirt worm in India

Lix: A beating

Mamee: Mother's brother's wife

Maticoor: A female-centered ritual meant to instruct a bride to be on sexual matters

Mamu: Mother's brother

Nani: Maternal grandmother

Pandit: A Hindu priest

Pepperpot: An Amerindian-derived stew popular in Guyana. It is traditionally served at Christmas

Phagwah: An annual Hindu Festival of Colours celebrating the arrival of Spring

Pickney: Creole word for 'child'

Ramayana: One of the two major Sanskrit epics of ancient Indian history

Ram Leela: Hindu tradition that takes place every year before Diwali

Soca: A genre of music that uses Afro-Caribbean rhythms of traditional calypso with the music of India and dancehall beats

Steups: A gesture of annoyance or disapproval

Skunt: A word in the Guyanese culture used as an expletive/curse word

Tassa: Kind of drum

Acknowledgements

When this idea first came to mind, we were a month into the COVID-19 pandemic. At home, with more spare time than I knew what to do with, I turned to the ample unread books on my shelf. Two of these books were anthologies; *Trinidad Noir* and *Jahaji: An Anthology of Indo-Caribbean Fiction*. Through these books, I was acquainted with a number of Caribbean authors I hadn't known before. I loved that each story gave me a sense of the writers' voice and style, all while capturing pieces of our culture. I went on a binge of Caribbean literature after that, wanting to get my hands on everything. That being said, first and foremost, I want to show my deepest appreciation for the Indo-Caribbean storytellers that have come before me. They have paved the way for us, showcasing our culture and stories to the world and giving voice to our community. For that, I'm forever grateful and inspired.

To each of the writers (Ashley, Saira, Kamala, Anna, Alexandra, Tiffany, Alyssa, Savita, Natasha, Karimah, Suhana, Krystal, Jihan, Mari, and Alya) who contributed to this book, I can't thank you all enough for sharing your work with me and trusting my vision for this book. From reading each of your stories, I've learned more about your writing styles, voices and have such a deep appreciation for the messages that are in each piece. I know each of you put your heart into your writing, and your stories have a special place in my heart. Thank you for helping me make this dream a reality.

To my talented cover artist, Chelsi, thank you for being so enthusiastic about this project and bringing my vision to life. Your design was even better than I imagined and even though I've told you countless times how beautiful it is, know that I'm amazed every time I look at the book. I'm grateful for your patience and understanding throughout the process.

To each of the readers, I'm so grateful for each of you. Thank you for supporting this book and showing myself and the contributors so much love. I sincerely hope you enjoyed each of the stories, were able to relate to the narratives and found comfort in the characters.

To the Indo-Caribbean community, thank you for inspiring me each and every day. I love waking up every morning and seeing Indo-Caribbean faces, creativity and history on my timeline. You all do such wonderful things and think it speaks volumes to the beauty and resilience in our culture and our people. I hope we will never stop striving to grow and carry on this legacy.

To my parents, Adrian and Sabita, thank you for fostering my love of reading and taking the time to read my work and ask questions. Thank you for helping me with my research and sharing stories about our family with me. Much of my writing is inspired by your stories, your experiences, your childhoods. I'm forever grateful for your support, your love, your sacrifices.

To my little brother, Jalen, thank you for being you, for brightening my days, for giving the best hugs.

To Yvano, my love, thank you for supporting me and this project from start to finish. Your positivity, encouragement and love has always made the good days better and the dark days brighter. I'm grateful to have shared so much of this journey with you and look forward to everything that is to come for both of us.

About the Editor

Tiara Jade Chutkhan is a book blogger, writer and editor born and raised in Toronto. Her love of literature led her to start blogging and sharing her reads, particularly those by BIPOC authors. Through her blogging, Tiara has had the opportunity to review books for HarperCollins, Penguin Random House, and ZG Stories.

Tiara's Indo-Caribbean heritage is extremely important to her and she strives to create representation for her community. Her writing is focused on exploring the Indo-Caribbean diaspora, its history and culture as well as community features.

Tiara is the Editor-in-Chief at The Brown Girl Diary and the Marketing Coordinator at Diaspora Dialogues. She is a regular contributor for The Brown Girl Diary and Caribbean Collection Magazine. Tiara is also working towards a certificate in Creative Writing from University of Toronto.

Two Times Removed: An Anthology of Indo-Caribbean Fiction is her first book.

❀ Connect Online: ❀

www.tiarajade.com

@bookwormbabee

About the Contributors

Ashley Anthony is a hospital pharmacy technician and freelance editor. When not working, they can be found reading, baking, or practicing their creative skills in different art media. You can check out their work on Instagram (@tripleawesomeart) where they share baking adventures, as well as various art projects they have worked on - including a completed One Hundred Day Project (#100DaysofStickyNoteStories).

Saira Batasar-Johnie locates herself as a brown, Indo-Caribbean Canadian cisgender womxn of Indo Caribbean/South Asian Indian descent and 1st generation settler in T'karonto/Toronto, Ontario situated on the territory of the Anishinaabe, Mississaugas of the New Credit and Haudenosaunee Peoples, with recognition to "The Dish With One Spoon" wampum and Treaty 13. Saira's family were immigrants escaping violence and oppression in Guyana and Trinidad. Why this is important for her to recognize this with you is because understanding colonization and our history, starts here, starts in the conversations we have and the notion that we will not continue to reproduce the history that has destroyed many indigenous families. Saira is a Child and Youth Care Worker as well as a mom, wife, daughter, sister and friend. Saira is passionate about bringing the history of Indo-Caribbeans to the newest diaspora of young people. She hopes to educate young people with her words and inspire them to continue their journey of understanding self in this world.

Alexandra Daignault is the owner and founder of Sarjesa, working behind the scenes on the operational and social impact pieces. She is an experienced activist and community organizer focused on social enterprise and community development spaces. She has completed the ASHOKA - AMERICAN EXPRESS bootcamp for emerging leaders, and has been the recipient of numerous awards - speaking at conferences and facilitating workshops across North America. Graduating as the valedictorian of her class, Alexandra is focused on creating more equitable and safe spaces for marginalized women across communities.

Kamala Chan Singh is an Indo-Guyanese creative currently living in Queens, New York with her husband. She immigrated to the United States with her family at the age of four. She enjoys reading, writing, painting, photography and cooking (amongst many other hobbies). In June of 2020, Kamala was inspired to create her Bookstagram account after noticing the lack of representation in the Indo-Caribbean community. She wanted to create a safe space online where people of similar backgrounds could feel seen and understood through her reflections. It was imperative for her to build a strong community of BIPOC creators. In her professional life, she works as a Licensed Skincare Therapist, specializing in acne and hyperpigmentation treatments. One of her passions is reclaiming the sacred practices of Yoga and Meditation. Kamala is currently building a luxury wellness brand set to launch in 2021. If you'd like to check out her book reviews and reflections, follow her Instagram @readwithkamala.

Anna Chowthi lives in Toronto, Canada after immigrating from Guyana with her family when she was 3 years old. She is Founder and Principal Project Leader of Merge Projects, a Technology Project Management Consultancy, Creator and Writer at Woman: Accomplished, a platform dedicated to women on their journey to their highest selves, and Co-Creator of Savouring the Indo-Caribbean, a platform dedicated to sharing, educating and celebrating Indo-Caribbean culture through food and nutrition. She was born on October 22, 1989 and comes from a family of three siblings with five nieces and nephews. She accredits her ambition and motivation—whether it would be in business leadership, lifestyle or her creations—to the support of the loving human beings around her and her commitment to wellness. Some of which include meditation, yoga, journaling and various Ayurvedic practices. She's an adventure traveller, Caribbean food lover, and nature enthusiast.

Jihan Ramroop is an Indo-Guyanese American writer and actress born in Queens, New York and raised in Fort Pierce, Florida. She is a graduate of SUNY Purchase College's Theatre and Performance program. Jihan's poetry memoir, "we used to waitress," is available now. Instagram: @weusedtowaitress

Tiffany Manbodh was born and raised in Guyana then migrated to the United States at the age of 9. Her childhood was filled with books and traveling along the border of Guyana and Brazil to a place known as Lethem. She is incredibly passionate about empowering other women to share their stories through the written word, having published a poetry book that explores trauma and healing. Her background is in Education so it's no surprise that she has a strong desire for continuous learning. Tiffany recently began her journey as a Health Coach and will be sharing it on her social media platforms. Her mission is to educate and empower women to take charge of their health from a holistic perspective. She is also an advocate for mental health and gender based violence within the Caribbean community and continues to raise awareness around such prevalent topics on social media.

Alyssa Mongroo is a law student at New England Law | Boston. She has a Bachelors in Criminal Justice from Marist College. Born into a Trinidadian family and living in upstate New York, Alyssa was no stranger to imposter syndrome. Through her writing, she has strived to promote diversity in the legal field by bringing to light the gaps between getting a legal education and coming from a West Indian home. Alyssa also has a makeup and fashion blog, www.alyssamongroo.com. She has partnered with brands such as MiniLuxe, Pixie Beauty, and Solara Suncare. You can check out her instagram @alyssamongroo.

Natasha Persaud works in the Child and Youth Care field. She is a recent graduate from Sherdian college. Natasha was born and raised in Canada, and is of Trinidadian and Guyanese heritage. She embraces both cultures proudly and is always willing to learn more about her cultures when she can. Natasha is the youngest of four siblings. When Natasha is not writing, she is reading, cooking, painting or binge watching Netflix. Her passions include advocating for mental health, and bringing out the confidence in people. She is determined to make a positive difference in anyone's life who she comes across.

Savita Prasad was born and raised in the borough of Queens in the state of New York. Growing up, she realized the Indo-Caribbean/ West Indian culture is a unique category that has not been defined yet and is at risk for extinction. As a kid, she loved asking members of the older generation questions and listening to the stories they had to offer. After graduating from CUNY Hunter College with a Bachelors degree in Biological Sciences and Psychology, she is currently pursuing the field of medicine to achieve the larger goal of taking care of people in her community. An advocate for representation and gender equality, social justice concerns are close to her heart. She is a skincare-junkie and has recently taken an interest in products for curly hair. In her free time, she enjoys hiking, ziplining, taking naps, and Netflix-ing.

Karimah Rahman founded *The Muslim Indo-Caribbean Collective* (MICC @muslimindocaribbeancollective) and *The Muslim Indentureship Studies Center* (MISC @muslimindenturestudiescenter). She is pursuing her PhD in Policy Studies on the intersectional marginalization, lack of representation and Anti-Muslim Racism towards Muslim Indo-Caribbeans (and marginalization of Indo-Caribbeans) in policy (India's Diaspora Policy and Ontario's 2001 South Asian Heritage Act), Indo-Caribbean, Indentured Diasporic, Indian and South Asian spaces due to problematic 'purity/authenticity' politics. She coined *The South Asian/Indian "Authenticity/Purity" Hierarchy Theory*, *Mainland South Asian Privilege* and *Indian/Indo-Caribbean Privilege* to unpack this. Karimah looks at the legacy of Muslim Indo-Caribbean resistance to colonization, journey of learning/unlearning, intergenerational trauma (rooted in Indentureship, colonization, white supremacy, Hindu supremacy, Hindutva ideology, Brahmin supremacy etc.) and decolonizing (including Mental Health). Karimah is a published author with work ranging from academic to spoken words, she has given talks, interviews and workshops on the topics mentioned.

Alya Somar is an up and coming writer from Mississauga, Ontario. A love for both reading and writing since an early age has fuelled her talent, as well as creativity. Being the daughter of two Guyanese immigrants is an integral part of her identity as she continues to carve out space for Caribbean writing in Canadian Literature, and more. Alya is currently pursuing an honours bachelor's degree in Creative Writing and Publishing at Sheridan College.

Suhana K. Rampersad is a poet and writer of Trinidadian descent. After completing the Creative Writing program at York University in Toronto, she took her talents to Instagram and developed a poetry page where she shares poems grounded in culture, feminism, love, and womanhood. She has written for Caribbean Collective Magazine, The Brown Girl Diary, and hosted the web show "French Fun with a Caribbean Twist" in association with A Different Booklist Cultural Centre on Facebook live. Suhana is currently pursuing a Bachelor of Education, with the goal of becoming a teacher who empowers young people through learning. Her other hobbies include baking and dancing, having trained in Indo-Caribbean dance styles since the age of five. As a first-generation West Indian Canadian, she hopes to use writing as a means to preserve heritage and history, and to highlight the experiences of Indo-Caribbean women everywhere.

Mari "Dev" Ramsawakh is a disabled, non-binary and Indo-Caribbean-Canadian multidisciplinary artist and storyteller. Born to Guyanese and Trinidadian parents, they were born and raised in the suburbs outside of Toronto. Their work focuses on their many intersecting identities and social justice. They have written news articles, essays, and opinion pieces for CBC, HuffPost Canada, Insider, Bitch Media, and other publications. They have produced the podcasts Sick Sad World and Cripresentation, and have acted as editor for Possibilities Podcast and Leaders in Colour Podcast. They've been published short fiction in the 2014 Hart House Review and in the Toronto 2033 anthology published by Spacing Magazine. They also facilitate workshops on ableism and anti-oppression, write poetry and occasionally model.

Krystal M. Ramroop, better known as Krys, is an innovative American born Indo-Guyanese writer and aspiring professional film and television actress. A first-generation summa cum laude and Phi Beta Kappa graduate of the City University of New York's City College (CCNY), Krystal's a music, film, and tea junkie at heart and hopes her curiosity and niche for cross-cultural writing will allow her to share her research and experiences and create a realm for readers to join her in. She also enjoys reading, watching cricket and soccer, singing and dancing to her favorite Caribbean and Indian tunes, and dabbling in photography. With upcoming releases in Caribbean anthologies, her writings have been featured in Promethean Literary Journal and online for her WordPress website, The Art of Storytelling, Akashic Books' Flash Fiction Duppy Series, Brown Girl Magazine, Avaaz Media, and Brown Sugar Literary Magazine.

Until next time.

Made in the USA
Monee, IL
30 May 2021